Praise for previous Greg M. Sarwa's writing

"Author Greg Sarwa's style has an ineffable quality that is the mark of great writing. Deceptively simple, his storytelling combines a poetic air with clear-eyed practicality…"

"…will keep the readers engrossed in the story right from the word go, filling them with suspense and a sense of anticipation as to what will happen next. This is a book not to be missed..."

BookWire Review

"…this story is well-written, action packed and easy to follow. Readers will enjoy the frenetic pace of the story with its fascinating twists and turns."

Dana Blozis, ForeWord CLARION reviews

"…runs a range of vibrant emotions without ever sinking into the maudlin or the melodramatic. It's a good, strong story which tugs at the heartstrings and at times tickles the funny bone…Well written, well paced and significantly insightful, Sarwa's novel is well worth reading."

M. Wayne Cunningham, ForeWord Magazine

"I guarantee that you will not be able to put down this novel once you begin to read it."

Alan Caruba, Editor, Bookviews.com

"Sarwa's writing is sprinkled with some vivid detail and his characters are nicely drawn and distinctive."

Norm Goldman, Bookpleasures.com

"Well-written and balanced in descriptive scenes, dialogue, and plot, it is a page-turner I didn't want to put down. But then, neither did I want the tale to end…"

"This novel is the best soul mate story I have ever read."

Heather Froeschl, Bookreviews.com

"Sarwa, of Northbrook, does a fine job of keeping the suspense hovering."

Joanne Zerkel, Star Newspapers

"…it's a soul-touching story that you will never forget."

Another Review at MyShelf.Com

"The best writing causes you to suspend your most fundamental principles of disbelief and that is what happened to me when I read this book."

Charles Ashbacher, Amazon Top 50 Reviewer

Books by Greg M. Sarwa:
The Cattle
If Only I could…

The Valley of Silent People

A Novel

Greg M. Sarwa

AMPOL PUBLISHING

The Valley of Silent People

ISBN 0-6157073-8-6
ISBN 978-0-6157073-8-9
Library of Congress Control Number 2012918408

First Printing November 2012
Printed in the United States of America

Cover photograph by Anna Sarwa

AMPOL PUBLISHING

This book is dedicated to my Mom and Dad.

The Valley of Silent People

Through the gates hollow gazes,
By the phrases floating in the shadows.
Through the eyes unable to witness,
By the thoughts yet to be conceived.

In the Valley of Silent People,
Children's names are being stolen,
In the Valley of Silent People,
Death glides with a silent roar.

Through the years streaming ahead,
In the rivers of our pure blindness.
Spinning life's square wheel of fortune,
I'll keep going, push forward, and…

In the Valley of Silent People,
Hope is sucked out by the gallons.
In the Valley of Silent People,
Last word just had lost its sound.

—*Maciej Danek*

Prologue

The ghostly breath slowed its furious dance over the unpaved road. It headed through a gate—a broken link in the pasture fence, unpredictably discarding another layer of pallid snow among the naked trees. Once it finished its last step around the other side of this garden of memories, it departed in perfect silence. Scattered brick and mortar dwellings, bitter gray monuments, and elaborate chapels pierced the paleness of the bare landscape to blend with the muddy horizon, ensuring that the solitude of souls wasn't compromised. Overshadowing the grounds, a concrete cross kept silent vigil from its lofty station, staring down at those who hurt the most.

The sound of snowshoes whispered over frozen ground in an erratic tap dance, as the small group tightened their circle, making sure nothing ventured out—or in. They stood on the small area of unplowed bare ground listening to the priest, his reddened hand sculpting the sign of the cross in the icy air. But listening to him wasn't an easy task for anyone, especially for Joe. The priest probably spent the whole morning in his little room at Saint Mary Magdalene Parish, just to ensure a well-received service. It was just his assumption; Joe didn't know him that well, though they had spoken casually after the few masses he was forced to attend. But those conversations were among the many small talks a priest was supposed to have with his parishioners—nothing special, nor important.

Joe Clatt motionlessly eyed into the bleak stretch of cemetery far behind the priest. His mind didn't react when the ceremony ended, and he was asked to throw the dirt into his wife's grave. Gradually, he realized that those few people present were waiting for him to make the first move. He tried, but he couldn't seem to make his body obey. His brain was set to the simple task, but there was no reaction, nothing; his own powerlessness silently cuffed him. Pete, his father-in-law, had to grasp Joe's hand and force him to take a fistful of dreary soil from the pile that rose next to them. Solid beached black dirt bit Joe's skin. With a soundless scream, he pulled his hand up and extended it over the grave. A plain pine coffin shone like a light in the endless mournful tunnel of earth. Joe's tears became hail, bruising his cheeks with the raw force. The thawing grime wrapped around his palm, his fingers reluctant to make the first and final throw. Again, Pete took charge by squeezing Joe's elbow. Each separate clod hitting the top of the casket sounded like the salvo of an execution squad.

After a while, Pete gently pushed him aside to make a room for the mourners who had come to say their last goodbye to Sally. Even if he could look up, Joe couldn't identify them anyway. Except his parents and Pete, he barely knew anybody here. Fox River Valley Gardens, a village thirty-five miles northwest of Chicago, was big enough for everyone to know each other, but it wasn't his place; it was Sally's. He had been here only a few times since they got married, but those trips weren't long enough to really get to know anyone. This time, though, it wasn't just a visit.

Joe remained by the grave with his hand extended to accept condolences while his consciousnesses drifted away into unknown realms. Automatically shaking hands with the people was all he could manage. No words came, and in a brief glimmer of perception, he felt guilty. He should show some gratitude to all those folks who arrived. But it was something Joe was not capable of doing. He could only acknowledge the presence of Pete and the priest who stood right next to him, and who politely thanked every one of the visitors on his behalf. As the last griever departed through the gloomy gate, the priest prepared himself to leave. He reached to place his hands over Joe's head, but stopped short when Joe took a sharp step back. He spoke no words, or expressed surprise, but a soft sympathetic smile crossed the priest's face before he turned away.

Joe and Pete witnessed the freshly formed dismal pile within the innocent carpet of the snow. A few candles flickered, but their flames weren't strong enough to dispel the dimness or warm the heart.

"Let's go home," said Pete, taking Joe's hand again. "There is nothing we can do. Everything is in God's hands now."

Joe didn't answer. He stared at the coal-like dirt that had been hollowed out many hours before the burial. He was trying to find white inserts of snow in the soil he thought he saw earlier, but he didn't see them anymore. There was only a dark, withered mound covering the place where, only minutes ago, he had seen Sally for the last time.

"Joe? Are you—" said Pete.

"I know." said Joe.

"What?" Pete's voice broke. "What did you say?"

"I know that there is nothing I can do." Joe glanced at Pete's face. "But there is nothing God can do either. Sally is dead. If there is God, why did He let it happen? If He was somewhere out there," Joe pointed toward the lifeless sky above, agitation grating in his voice, "he wouldn't let her die! Would He?" Joe paused, his huffs leaving a heavy fog in the cold air. "So—" Joe pulled his hand from Pete's grasp and walked away.

Pete chased Joe, heedless of the fact that the curved cemetery alley had become even glossier than before, but he couldn't catch up. Joe was already sitting in the car when Pete approached the gate.

Pete abruptly stopped before reaching the gateway. Once again, he took a quick look at the car, but all he saw was an ice-covered rear windshield. There was no movement, as if no spirit existed anywhere in the vicinity. Just a moment ago, as he turned on the last curve before the exit, he had caught a glimpse of soft light, a gentle beam finding its way through the night, and he just wanted to make sure he was right. Far on the other side of the cemetery, a shimmer of light grew brighter with every second, the view partially covered by leafless trees.

At moments, Pete could see a crowd gathering and slowly moving toward the center. He could distinguish people holding thin candles in their hands marching in silent procession; one tall, heavy candle stole his attention as it radiated its power, soaring out of the sea of light. Pete could swear it was exactly in the center of the pulsating circle formed by all the smaller candles. The waves of light illuminated half of the cemetery and it seemed as if they would rip the darkness from this piece of the land. A weak smile flashed on Pete's face. He tried to fight off the tears, hidden just below the surface of the strong man façade he had been wearing this evening. Kneeling, he bowed his head, and made the sign of the cross, and then, glancing for the last time at the golden glow rising in the distance, he turned around and sped toward his car.

Chapter 1

I stood inside the room where Sally had spent all of her childhood and peered around. Everything was just the same as when I had seen it for the first time fifteen or more years ago. But at that moment, I had the impression that I was seeing it for the first time. After Sally moved out, Pete hadn't changed anything in her room. And neither had Sally. It was always her room; as far as she remembered, it had been this way, and she wanted to leave it untouched; the same yellowish wallpaper with a strange pattern of little red roses that grew around. I remembered the nights we laughed as we tried to figure out the designer's intention. A few times, we even went a little further and painted more roses in, just to make it stranger yet. Touching one of those painted roses, feeling its soft swell under my fingers, my eyes dry, it seemed that time itself stopped to cravingly listen.

I hardly noticed the paintings that hung on the wall over her small bed. Sally had taken her time to paint them, never rushing until she was sure she knew what she wanted to accomplish. She called them paintings of her love and life, but she never wanted to tell me why she had used so much red in them. I couldn't look at them anymore and turned away.

On the wooden nightstand that stood next to the bed, I could see a few of her personal items strewn around. I wanted to come closer but I felt as if the bed itself grabbed me by the throat and threw me at the yellow wall. The full-size bed was the same one she had slept in as a teenager. But later on, against my predictions, it turned out to be large enough to accommodate both of us when we were visiting her father. I always thought it was a very tight fit, but right then I would do anything to be able to get that close to her again. It was impossible. I knew that. Still, I imagined us in bed together again. For a brief moment, I nearly believed it was real. The feeling, the indescribable thirst for her presence, drained out my consciousness.

Deliberately, I approached her nightstand and studied the bits and pieces resting there. As always, they were all accounted for.

The small, fatigued marble pebble, a stuffed bear, his faded plush showing a lifetime of loving care, five tiny fragrance bottles, and the heart-shaped jewelry box.

"They are in the right place," said Sally when she moved out with me. "If I let them stay, they'll know I'll be back, that we will be back."

I didn't understand her at the time but went along with her. It was her treasure, and once she made her decision, it was out of the question—it was never to be changed. Not by me, not by anyone. But something out of place rested among these items, one additional piece that didn't belong here. I recognized it immediately because it was the only thing Sally always took with her. For some reason, the palm-sized ashen-yellow jar accompanied Sally wherever she went. She never left it anywhere. If she didn't hold it clutched in her hand, it was in her bag, or pocket, anywhere she could instantly reach for it. The jar was a gift from her mother, who had received it from her mother, a gift from her grandmother who had received it from her own mother as well.

According to Sally, it was a family tradition—a mother had transferred the jar to a daughter for generations. I remember asking her one time what would happen when a boy was born. Would he get a jar? Her lips formed a divine bloom, which always made my heart quiver. She said that, as far as she knew, there had been no boys born into her side of the family, so she had never given the matter any thought. I didn't want to hurt her feelings, but my masculinity just couldn't take that. Full of pride I explained that, scientifically speaking, the male determined gender, and my family ran greatly to boys rather than girls. I was sure we would have a boy. Sally didn't say anything as she smiled and kissed me…She had kissed me, and only now was I sure that her kiss was an apology to my ego, for she knew she would be right.

I found myself holding the jar—it seemed too new to be an heirloom—passed from generation to generation. But its appearance was deceiving—you would never find one like it in any antique store. And if it was as old as Sally had always claimed, it certainly was well cared for. I could imagine that much, since she had never let it out of her sight.

As I carefully placed it back on the nightstand, I overheard a voice coming from downstairs. I didn't want to eavesdrop but since the door was ajar, and Pete and his guest stood right under the stairs, temptation won over. I listened at the door.

"…We still don't know how that happened." I couldn't place the voice.

"But why?" asked Pete. "There has to be some kind of explanation."

"Believe me, I'm doing everything possible, but we've got nothing. It appears like something just swept them off the road..."

"A car?" It was more of a statement than a question. "There must be a trace of something. Chipped paint, tire treads, footprints...anything."

There was a long pause and then the unknown man sighed.

"Listen, Pete. We don't have anything. Not a clue. No traces of any car, no tire prints, not even one chip of paint—nothing whatsoever. The only witness—if you can call it a witness—was Brad, drunk as always, and...you know him—"

"Yes, I know him too well, but at least that's a start."

"What you are saying? He was probably born drunk. Hallucinating all his life—"

"Sally knew him," Pete's voice exhibited thin thread of hope. "He wasn't all that bad."

"Maybe not, but how can you even consider a story about a black object—he didn't say a car, and he wasn't even able to describe it—hitting them with such impact that Sally was killed instantly, thrown twenty yards off the road, and—"

"Is that what he said?" interrupted Pete. I sensed the tension in his voice. "Let's go to the kitchen. I'll make some coffee."

Their voices grew weaker. I lacked the courage to go downstairs and speak with them face-to-face, to ask them what the hell they were talking about. And I even had less desire to snoop on them talking in the kitchen. I stumbled back to the nightstand, grabbed the jar, and stretched out on Sally's bed. It was so warm, so imbued with her scent, that I buried myself in my thoughts, and time lost its meaning. I wasn't thinking about anything in particular; I just lay down with my eyes closed, searching for a shield that would protect me against the world awaiting me out there.

The murmur of voices drifted up the stairwell again, but then the heavy front door opened and shut. When I heard intense footfalls and the creaking of the wooden steps, I jumped up and sat on the edge of the bed. There was no knock before the door swung open on squeaky hinges, revealing Pete's bear-like form.

"Ah, here you are," he said. "I thought that you might come down. I wanted to introduce you to the chief of police. He's an old friend of mine. He came by to give us some details."

"And?" I said, holding back all of my questions and trying not to reveal that I had overheard part of their conversation.

"They don't know much. However, they are investigating. It's just too early to say anything."

"How it could be?" I said. "Why are they so slow? It's been what? What is it? The fourth or fifth day since the accident?"

"But they aren't sure how it had happened yet. They're trying to reconstruct—"

"Do they, at least, have any idea about the car responsible?"

"No, they're still searching." Pete avoided my eyes and focused on the wall behind me. I turned around to see what held his attention. Besides Sally's paintings against the yellow wallpaper, I couldn't see anything else.

"Somehow I don't see how that can be possible," I said. "I'm curious, Pete. How many cars do you have here? A hundred. Two maybe? Can't they just check all of them? How long would it take? A day or two?"

"Joe," the calmness of Pete's voice fueled my mounting fury. "It could be any car, not necessarily one from here. Someone could just be passing by—"

"I know," I said, making sure I hid my frustration. "But when you say that the police don't have a clue about what happened, I find it very, very strange."

"There are many things in this world that seem to be too extraordinary to be possible," he said, watching the wall behind my back. "So many you wouldn't believe. All we can do is accept the fact that God has His purpose."

"Oh, really?" My circuits overloaded. "And what kind of purpose would He have to kill my wife?"

Pete cringed at my blunt remark. "I don't know. Joe," he said, bowing his head. "I don't know, but whatever His purpose, it will reveal itself. Remember, Sally was also my daughter—I am grieving too."

I looked at him. From my position on the bed, he seemed even bigger that he truly was. In the murkiness of the room, I searched for his eyes. I couldn't find them. It looked as if he didn't have eyes at all. At that moment, I noticed that he had closed them. I understood that speaking of the death of his own daughter was as painful to him as my thoughts of my wife. I don't know whose pain was more immense, but until now, I had selfishly assumed that I was the only one who loved Sally. "What are we going to do now, Pete?" I said.

He didn't move, but his eyes opened.

"Actually I was thinking about going to bed. I am too tired," he said. "And I bet you are, too—this whole day must have been exhausting for you." He skimmed around the room.

"Do you think you want to sleep here?" he asked after a while.

"That's what I was thinking." I stood up and walked around Pete to turn the ceiling lights on. "If you don't mind. "I added.

"No, not at all." He paused. "If you want, I'll move your suitcase from the guest room—I didn't know how you...but this is as much yours as it was Sally's, so it's up to you."

"Thanks. I can handle it. I don't have much stuff anyway."

"So, you found it?" said Pete, pointing at the alabaster jar I was holding.

"Sally kept that jar with her all the time." I said. "I hope I can have it."

"If truth be told, you shouldn't," said Pete.

"I...what?" I couldn't believe what I had just heard. "That was my wife's. Why..."

"That jar belonged to my wife," Pete stopped me before I said too much. "Like Sally, she kept it with her all the time, never left it... My wife received it from her mother, and her mother from hers. That jar sure doesn't seem to be, but it is very, very old. You wouldn't guess how old it is. It runs from one generation to the next, from mother to daughter."

"I know the story," I said. "Sally told me—"

"So you understand me now." I knew where he was getting at with this. "I think…no, I should say, I am sure that Sally would give it to Rosemary, to keep up with the tradition."

"But Rosie is—" I said.

"She is still alive!" said Pete. "So it should be hers."

"Of course. You're right," I said. I couldn't grasp why he was so determined but I got the point. "You know I'll give it to her, if she—"

"There is no 'if!'" Pete shook his head. "It's 'when.' You just have to believe that, Joe."

I observed him closely, searching for any sign of disappointment on his face. But there wasn't any, not even the slightest frown broke his countenance. Pete stood in front of me, proud and strong, and I could swear I felt a hint of hope. I knew that, for my own sake, I should take advantage of it, however tiny and weak that flame was. I had to live on it, or try at least. I had nothing to lose. Not anymore.

I knew that Pete was one of the very few people who could help me make it through. Not even my parents could—they were supportive as always—but their encouragement was limited. Right after the services ended, they were gone. They went back home to live in the enclosed fortress they had slowly built for themselves over the years. No one else had a key to their world, not even their own child. Sometimes I blamed them for their insulated lifestyle, but, on the other hand, I could almost see their intentions. Nobody could do them any harm as long as they stayed inside. The untamed rain forests around them didn't matter.

Of course, the official reason was my father couldn't leave the business for too long, but I knew it wasn't the truth. I wish they'd stayed, not even to talk but just to be with me. Their presence would have given me the support I craved. Hoping to live my life differently, I tried not to cocoon myself—at least that was what I'd always deemed. But in the end, who knew? Maybe I was like them after all. But being with Sally made me open up, even if only a little. I wasn't sure anymore. What I thought I wanted most at that moment was to stay with Pete and talk. Talk about anything, just to be in his presence. But just as I was about to ask Pete to stay, another thought threw itself violently.

"I think I'm going to take a walk," I said before I had a chance to change my mind, and I handed the jar to Pete. "You better keep it."

"No, no," he said. "Let's put it back over here." He placed the jar back on the nightstand with the jewelry box and the worn plush bear. "It will wait here for the right moment."

"Are you sure?"

"Of course." He scrutinized me. "Where do you think you are going at this hour?" he asked.

"I have a feeling that I have to do this."

"Do you really want to go there? Right now?" Pete sighed. "Are you sure?"

"I think I am. I feel like I have to."

"What do you expect to see there?"

"I don't know," I said truthfully.

"It's almost nine, you won't be able to—"

"Pete, it doesn't matter—I have to."

"Do you want me to go with you?" he asked, looking straight into my eyes. His stare was so deep that I virtually felt his eyes boring inside my brain.

"No, I don't think so," I said as softly as I could. "I think I have to do it alone."

"Just say the word and I'll go along."

"No, Pete. Thanks." I moved toward the door.

"Well then, I think I'll go to bed." He turned but stopped abruptly. "I can wait for you, if you want."

"Don't wait, please. It's not necessary—I'll manage."

"It's up to you." He surrendered, and I was sure he finally understood that, even if it wasn't the greatest idea for me to go out at this moment, he couldn't stop me. "Do you have the key?"

"No, I forgot to grab it. I was so disoriented—"

"There's still a spare one outside. You know where?"

"I do." In fact, we had always used the spare key to Pete's house. Sally lost her own long ago, but she never admitted to it. So whenever we visited him, the spare key came in handy.

"Well, then. Good night."

An Arctic blast just about made me come back home from the poorly lit ice rink that should have been a street. It was short and narrow, a barely recognizable straight street peppered with a few houses at the far end of the village. Wide enough to accommodate two people walking side by side, there were sidewalks on both sides of the street, which lasted for only a few hundred yards or so. Tonight it didn't matter, they were useless—both covered by pillows of snow. The street itself invited me to travel its iced heart.

It had happened on their way to the church, just a few minutes' walk from Pete's house. Sally always hated to use the car when she was here; she was accustomed to walking since her childhood. Back then, people used cars only for long trips outside the village. She walked everywhere—the weather was never a problem. She walked to the store, to visit someone, or just for the sake of walking, and she tried to promote the habit with everyone else. I wasn't always fascinated by her obsession with walking, but she tried her best to recruit me. She always said she thanked God for places like Fox River Valley Gardens, where she could safely walk the street without any fear that some berserk car, like those murderous hit-and-runs in the city, would decide to run her over. That thought hurt physically—mercilessly severing my flesh. She thought she was safe here, and now what?

I walked the streets of the shadowy village without meeting even a soul on my way. When the swept sidewalk amazingly appeared at my side, I gladly acknowledged its presence. Since no car lights cut through the darkness of the night, I felt secure on the deserted street, but still, the sidewalk was much more comforting than the middle of the road. Widely spread streetlights wore snow caps, which caused the light to diffuse the frozen atmosphere of the late January night. But they were nowhere close to making my way any easier.

In less than ten minutes of the crunching march, the sidewalk ended. The lonely tower of the Saint Mary Magdalene Church should come into view behind the next curve, I recalled. The next curve—my heart seemed to stop, blood ceased flowing through my system. I was sure I could just take it out, iced up and lifeless, and my body wouldn't notice it missing. But then it burst into a gallop, pumping blood with supernatural power. I couldn't hear anything besides the roar of my blood rushing through my veins. I wasn't sure if I wanted to go any farther. Surely, anyone in the vicinity could hear the wild beating of my heart.

I turned around to see if anyone else could hear this one-man concert; the stage was empty. I was cold and started to wonder how long it would take to thaw my toes. Finally, the stings increasing with every step, I moved ahead; my eyes focused on the unknown ahead at the next curve.

I didn't have to search for it at all. The site, sacred only to me, lay visible from the distance. I was unsure of what I was doing. What was I searching for? I had no idea what I wanted to accomplish, but I knew that I had to see it. I had to be here now because I wasn't here when it happened. Scanning the curve, eyes roving from one end to the other, I admitted to my greatest mistake. It was too dark to see, and there were no lights anywhere close enough to give the slightest glimmer. Of course, I didn't have a flashlight with me. I never even thought of that.

Nevertheless, I proceeded anyway. Afraid of accidentally falling and defiling this holy ground, I carefully moved to the center of the large rectangular shape drawn by yellow police tape tied to the trees. There has been a wide soaring tree standing just inside. It was the only one not flagged, and I knew right away, that was the one. I just knew it. I couldn't help myself—I had to touch it. I embraced it fearfully, as though it was the last human being left on the planet. Its bark was surprisingly warm, its edges soft, when I slid down to sit by the huge, bulky roots. Only when I was on my knees, bent in half, with my face close to the ground, was I able to see the damage. Some of its sturdy roots were ripped from the ground, mangled and chewed by the teeth of the unknown predator—silent marks of whatever had happened here. Even the fresh snow wasn't able to conceal it.

Instinctively I raised my head and glanced toward the road. Its savage curve edged into a quiet forest glade. I was not more than twenty feet from the middle of the arch. How long? Seconds? Something broke inside. I couldn't hold it any longer, but it wasn't a cry. I howled. I promised myself that I would find out who had done this evil deed, and I would kill him. In cold blood, I would simply destroy the murderer, paying no heed to its cries for forgiveness. Nothing mattered to me anymore—I wanted the revenge. That unexpected feeling was born instantly but I knew it would stay alive until satisfied, until the blood of the killer stained my hands.

I heard a crack. Or I thought I heard it. I wasn't sure but something made a noise loud enough to silence my inner scream. A branch cracked again and in that split second, something moved close by. The noise indicated someone's uneven steps, the sound coming from inside the forest. Breathlessly I listened and finally pinpointed the exact direction. It seemed that someone was approaching me, but then abruptly the footsteps stopped. A slight gust of the bitter air brought a delicate salty-peppery scent, reminding me more of the sunny seacoast than the Siberian zone I was in. It was quiet for a few minutes before I decided to move. I was sure that the killer's guilty conscience had made him return to the scene of his crime, and I was blinded more by my hate and thoughts of revenge than the blackness around me. I strode in the direction where I had heard the last crack.

I saw the cause of the noise as I passed another tree close by. The contour of the man was even more sinister than the night. He sat on the snow with his back leaning against the trunk of the tree, rocking back and forth like an old riding horse. His head kept falling down amid his attempts to fight gravity. I didn't need to come any closer to find out who it was. The smell told me everything. Standing a few feet from the quivering man, I was sure he hadn't wasted his resources on water for a long time.

My first thought was to walk away, to leave him here to die in the cold, but even with that flame of hate growing inside of me, I couldn't do it. Judging by his condition, he would freeze to death out here in the woods before morning. He couldn't walk any longer, and it was only thanks to the tree that he wasn't lying down in the snow. I wondered if someone was out there looking for him...if he had family, wife, kids. What if he doesn't have anyone? What if no one is searching for the poor bastard, and he really will die? I wasn't convinced, but I couldn't just leave him here. I knew there was a church nearby, so I thought somehow I would carry him there and ask for help. At least it's going to keep me from staying here any longer, I thought.

I squatted, his head swung back and forth, spreading the fermented odor. Careful not to frighten him, I reached out.

"No accident—" I sprang back when I heard his sad gurgle before I touched him. His eyes were open now, but I had a feeling that he didn't see me. He stopped rocking and observed the dimness.

"What did you say?" I asked as I knelt again, this time right in front of him. He remained silent for a while. I was sure that it was my tired imagination playing games with me, and decided to proceed. I nearly laid my hand on his arm.

"No accident—must go there." I didn't see his mouth moving but his ominous voice surprised me so much, I fell back on the cushion of the snow.

"What is going on here?" I shouted, rising to my feet. "Is it some kind of a joke? If it is—you really are brainless. Stop it! Who are you? Why are you playing with me?" I didn't get any response. With his eyes closed now he was rolling back and forth against the trunk of the tree, just like before.

What is going on? I thought. Am I losing it?

Scared as a kid left alone in the long, dark night when all the nightmares come alive, I was ready to run away from this peculiar place. Instead, determination to help that man dominated my conscience. So one more time, I approached him, set to lift him off the ground, no matter what. Again, I didn't even touch him—I didn't have a chance. All of a sudden, his eyes shot wide open, gleaming eyeballs orbiting around like a lantern. I could see bulging veins, ready to burst, pumping the red fuel furiously. He turned his face to me, his breath so intense, I could barely stand it. The stench of teeth, unwashed for weeks and treated with vodka-based mouthwash, overwhelmed me. I turned my head to the side. With great effort, he pulled one hand up, right in my face.

"Must go there," he gurgled again. But I wasn't scared anymore. I took a close look at his old damaged face, and thin hoary lips, now zipped tight. His eyes calmed again, staring somewhere behind me, into the woods. It seemed like someone took the batteries out of him when he leaned back against the tree, transfixed. At that moment, my sixth sense must have sent me a signal that I could be in a danger. I wasn't sure what kind of danger it could be—it didn't say; it just dispatched an initial warning. My brain worked feverishly on possible escape routes. I steeled myself for yet another of his outbreaks. But I heard no more voices, not a word. He leaned against the tree, peacefully, quietly. With my last bit of courage, I turned my head to see what he could possibly see there. Maybe it is still behind me. His eyes! He was afraid. But I didn't spot anything except the solid ebony curtain surrounding the woods and me. I decided to resolve this strange situation immediately by waking him up, and getting us both out of here. But when I turned my head back—he was…gone.

The acid coldness of the night felt like a subtle breeze compared to the icy pangs of panic running through my whole body.

With trembling hands, I patted the tree in front of me, its coarse bark bruising my palms through my gloves. I yanked my head around, but as far as I could see, he wasn't there anymore. He had sublimated. I analyzed the last couple of minutes. When I turned around, he was by the tree, drunk as a sailor on the first night in port. When I looked back, he was gone. What the hell is this? I swear I didn't hear any noises. He had to make a noise when he moved. In his condition, hell, the whole woods would wake up if he moved. I was more and more certain that something was not right over here. Either I am going insane or... or...

"No accident, you must go there," his voice sounded in my head again. And I knew I was going crazy. Then another thought hit my troubled and scared mind. When I realized what he meant, a slow numbing wave started from the bottom of my feet and moved straight up my spine. I knew it! It took some time but I finally got the message. With all my heart, I fought my stiff body, forcing it to move ahead.

"Rosemary," I screamed and hurried in the general direction of the road, oblivious to the deep, icy snow, and the broken branches in my way. "Rosie!"

Chapter 2

I could hear Pete's old-fashioned tube TV while fighting with the door lock. It was much louder than my usual comfortable reception level—I had totally forgotten he liked it that way. When I finally burst through the door, I found him sitting in the slightly worn-out recliner, hands resting on his lap. I caught sight of a bit of tan paper sticking out from under his tired hands, though his wide palms hid the rest of it. His head leaned to the side but only a little, as if afraid to come fully to rest itself on his shoulder. His chest moved up and down in a slow, continuous rhythm. Pete had pulled the armchair close to the small fireplace, to within inches of the TV, claiming the whole screen for himself. He sat at rest, oblivious to my arrival. I edged close enough to touch his shoulder and wake him up. His eyes snapped open, as though he wasn't napping at all, but was fully aware of his bearings. It appeared that he had waited for me, fully dressed with his shoes still on, and a heavy woolen coat neatly draped on the sofa. He examined me for a moment, and then turned off the TV.

"You don't look good, Joe," he said. "What happened?" The calmness of his voice wrapped itself snuggly around my tired psyche, while I fought the urge to shout out what had happened back there in the woods, from the drunken man to the strange words he uttered. Somehow, I held back.

"We have to go to the hospital." I surprised myself that I could state it so serenely.

"What's with your pants?" He whispered, and pointed to my legs. "What did you do there? And your jacket? It looks like someone beat you with a stick. What happened to you?"

"Nothing," I said, glancing down at my body to estimate the damage. It wasn't that bad. My pants were wet below the knees, and now, since Pete had mentioned it, I felt melted snow soaking my boots and socks. I appraised my jacket—it had only a few scratches on the sleeves; the rest was just dirt.

"It was so dark, I couldn't see where I was going. I just slipped a few times. That's all." I said, trying to avoid his eyes.

"You're OK, then?" It didn't sound like a question. "Well, why the hospital?"

"Rosie," I said. "I have to see Rosie."

"Isn't it too late now? Besides, we were just there before the funeral. Tell me, why do you want to go there at this hour?"

"I just have to see her. I have to make sure she's OK."

"She is, Joe." He sounded so convincing that, if I didn't know him better, I would say he was a priest. He had the same persuasive tone to his voice, the one that made sinners want to beg for forgiveness.

"I have to go." Not giving up, I took a few steps back, toward the door. "I just need to see Rosemary. Are you going with me?" I paused. "If not, just let me borrow your car, please."

Pete rose from the comfort of his armchair holding a tan envelope in his hands. "I thought that I'd give this to you. It's a—"

"Not now, Pete. It can wait," I said, already halfway out the door.

"OK then, let's go. I hope they'll let us in." He turned back, and placed the envelope on the coffee table. Then he was right behind me.

The Lutheran General Hospital was located some fifteen minutes' drive from the village, encircled by an enormous vacant plain, right in the heart of nowhere. But the location was deceiving. It was one of the better hospitals in the whole state; at least that was the consensus. Whether it was true or not, three wings of the hospital building seemed unnaturally empty right now. Several windows, lit by fluorescent light that penetrated vertical blinds, formed the sign of a shattered cross on the obscure exterior wall.

It was already well after ten when we walked in. The security officer sat behind the desk in the large reception area. He was an older man who wore his security uniform with a pride that would put some soldiers to shame. He smiled softly and waved us through without asking any question. Nobody hindered us along the way or commented on our late visit.

We walked through the deserted hallways, trying not to spoil the perfect composure of this place; but inside my head rang the clear strains of inert music, a symphony created by the overwhelming tranquility. We rode the elevator up to the fourth floor and ran into another set of plain corridors. Somewhere in the middle of the maze, behind a glass door of the ICU unit, we found another reception desk. A nurse, in her dreary blue outfit, kept watch. She used the computer screen to shield her face, as though she deemed she should have a better report for us.

"Nothing has changed. I'm sorry," she whispered, giving us permission to proceed to Rosie's room.

A wave of relief rolled over me as we walked softly down the hall. It wasn't huge, but it was enough to calm me just a little. "Nothing has changed." So the drunken guy was wrong, he was mistaken! No—there was no drunken guy; it was just my imagination. I need some rest. But that brief moment of relief clouded as the "nothing has changed" sentence crept up on me again. It means Rosie is in the same condition, no better, no improvement. I wasn't sure what to think about that, and began analyzing the night's encounter all over again. Our arrival at Rosie's door interrupted my thoughts.

It seemed that everything that night was painted in varying shades of black. The small, darkened room seemed bare in the faint illumination of one dim nightlight, its tedious walls and flooring more suited to an autopsy room. Even a leather recliner, and a little coffee table thrown in there with hope to mitigate the ambiance, failed to perform their duty. Some polished metal shelving, and two carts fenced in my daughter. They held a vast array of medical equipment, most pulsating with angry lights, others beeping ghoulishly, sounds that only deepened the feeling of misery.

Rosemary rested peacefully in the sterile bleached bed; so calm. I wasn't sure if it was the meager lighting or if her olive skin had, in fact, darkened; it was so fresh and glowing amid the spider web of IV tubes and monitor cords. It didn't matter; she was beautiful, just like her mom. She was so like Sally. I was amazed. I felt that I was discovering my daughter for the first time. I had always known that Rosie would be an exact copy of her mom, but now, at eight, more than ever. Her long auburn hair curved and curled around her head in smooth brush strokes. For a moment, I wondered who had tended to her tonight. I was certain I hadn't asked anyone, but that thought disappeared as I looked at her closed eyes. I remembered them—brown, large, smart, forgiving eyes— eyes that held to the childish belief that the world was one big, happy, safe home. Those eyes trusted everyone, and never judged people. She was always trying to find their better sides, even those who committed the worst crimes. Sometimes I didn't know whose eyes were looking at me—my wife's or my daughter's—they were so alike. The sleeves of the hospital gown covered Rosie's arms to just above the elbows. I lay my eyes on her smooth hands, another resemblance, a tiny discoloration, a diamond-shaped coffee freckle between her right-hand thumb and the index finger—lifeless and faded, now. It appeared as if she was asleep; perhaps she dreamed, perhaps not.

Why would someone want to harm her? I thought. She is so innocent.

As I stared at my poor, inert daughter, I heard the door swing open and someone entered the room. Simultaneously, Pete and I turned our heads. It was the same doctor who admitted Rosie to the hospital right after the accident. When I saw him, I started to think about the counseling services that he had offered to introduce me to. The silver-haired, well-mannered gentleman had done all he possibly could, under the circumstances, to keep my spirits up. I was not sure to what extent he was successful but at least I appreciated his effort. For a moment, I thought that it wouldn't be a bad idea to attend few sessions. After all, it wouldn't hurt me. But then, just the thought of sharing my personal feelings with strangers gave me shivers, and I dismissed the idea. I was sure no one would understand me; everyone would try to be a judge. I would just make a fool of myself.

The doctor approached Rosie and glanced through a display of lethargic monitors.

"Mr. Clatt and Mr. Roberts. How may I help you?" he said, one hand stroking his frosted beard. "I was leaving when I heard that you had arrived. Is there any particular reason you have decided to visit Rosemary at this hour?"

Pete turned his head toward me and nodded.

"Nothing really, I was...I was really uneasy about Rosie, that's all." I said. "I just wanted to see her again, tonight. I don't know...maybe I hoped—"

"As I told you before, Mr. Clatt," the doctor said with authority, "there is not much we can do at this time. You see...She...hm... Rosie is perfectly fine as far as I can say. I mean from a medical standpoint. There is nothing wrong with her, not a thing. Each organ is functioning properly; she is a young and healthy girl. We have run every possible test and examination, and we haven't found anything out of the ordinary. On the charts everything seems to be normal—"

"Then, what is wrong?" I had heard this spiel over and over again. "Why can't you just find what—" I stopped, afraid that I would say something unkind.

"Rosie isn't reacting to the outside world," he pointed toward the bed. "She is in a coma-like state, but for now her brain is working properly. There is no reason for her condition as it is right now. As a doctor with almost thirty years of experience, I have never seen a case like hers. I have consulted with a few of the top neurologists in the world, and even they don't have any answers. Actually, I am waiting for three of my colleagues—maybe four, if she can make it from England. Rosie's condition is so rare, I'm sure she will not want to miss the opportunity to examine her. They wanted to see her—"

"When will she wake up?" I knew I had asked that same question over and over. He probably had had enough of my dogged determination, but I couldn't stop myself from asking.

"As I have told you before, Mr. Clatt, there is no answer to that. It could be a day, two, or a month, a couple of—"

"Or never," I finished his sentence.

"Don't you ever say that again, Joe," Pete scolded. "She is the most precious thing we have. We have to keep faith. We can't ever abandon her—"

"I didn't say I want to abandon her, Pete. I was only—"

"Mr. Roberts is right, Mr. Clatt." This time the doctor interrupted me. "You must not give up hope. Pray and—"

"Pray?" I probably would have said something very stupid, but Pete cut in.

"Some people would call it a prayer, some—meditation, others a dialog with the inner self. In reality, it doesn't matter what you call it. The truth is the truth; in the end, everybody is searching for the same thing. Do you agree, doctor?"

"I couldn't have stated it better myself, Mr. Roberts," he said with a smile.

"So, Joe," Pete said as he turned to me, "don't feel offended by this, but just try to look inside yourself and find a measure of faith. Nobody is asking you to believe in something you don't want to. All you need, all any of us needs, is to have a little faith."

Have faith? I thought, as I glanced at my daughter, kept alive only by means of soulless medical machinery. I was powerless against the unknown and the unexplained, unable to even find out who had perpetrated such a terrible act against my family. I shouted, "Faith in what?" Then I left the room, not even capable of slamming the door behind me.

Chapter 3

The ride from the hospital was mute. Pete busied himself driving while I searched for a moon shadow and inhaled the dreariness outside the window. Finally, I caught a glimpse of the moon touching the ground with its ivory finger, but it lasted for only a few seconds. I felt a little guilty after realizing that Pete and the doctor had intended only to help me, but I wasn't in the mood to apologize yet. Frustrated and angry with everybody, including myself, I didn't want to cause more hurt than I already had.

We arrived back at the Pete's well after midnight. It helped me, but not as much as I expected it would. Without a word, we both stopped in the kitchen. Pete sank into a chair behind the square table. He must have sensed my hesitation, because he took the first step.

"Are you going to bed?" he said.

"I'll try," I said, struggling to hide my emotion. "Good night." I turned around with the intention of walking out. Since I arrived here, a couple of days before Sally's funeral, I'd stayed in the guest bedroom. Until this evening, I couldn't—wouldn't even consider occupying the Sally's room. It would probably be too much.

But tonight was different. I felt the overwhelming compulsion to be in her room, I knew she would want me to be there. I couldn't say no to Sally. She had taught me how to follow my instinct, and that was exactly was I was about to do.

"Wait a minute." The chair scratched the floor and Pete rushed in my direction. "Just a minute, please." He grabbed my hand.

"What happened?" I wasn't sure what had surprised me more—his quickness, or his iron grasp on my arm.

"Nothing. If you can just—just..." The last word hung suspended in the air, unspoken.

He appeared incapable of saying anything more than that. He stuttered, apparently unable to utter more than a peaceful hiss of half-said words that drifted about the room. What is it now? I thought. Hadn't I had enough for tonight?

"What's going on, Pete?" I said, finally putting the irritating noise to an end.

"Well—" I waited for the hiss again but Pete recouped and his voice returned to his normal, deep tone. "Do you think we can have a glass of beer?"

"Pete, you know I don't drink." I said, watching him closely. "You know me better." Not that I was a teetotaler from birth—I had my own share of the bottle, and just couldn't take it anymore. "What's up with you? Tell me."

"Let's sit down for a while," said Pete, then he walked out of the kitchen. Obediently, I went after him to the small family room with sofa and two recliners, one touching the TV now, arranged in the center, a cozy brick fireplace gracing one of the walls.

"Pete, we have time. Can't it wait until morning?" I said as he sat down in one of the armchairs. "I really want to go to bed now."

"It won't take long," he said and stood up again.

What is wrong with him tonight? I thought.

"Let me just grab a can and I'll be right back," he added. "Come on, sit down. It won't take long, I promise." He was gone.

I wasn't too happy about this. It seemed like yet another attempt at mutual family grieving, which I just couldn't stand the thought of. All that had needed saying had been said; there was nothing more left to add, but I didn't want to be an undocked moron and botch Pete again. He was my father-in-law, and no matter what disagreement we had, I wouldn't say that he wasn't a fine man. He had his difficult side, but who didn't have at least one complication. So, as exhausted I was, as unwilling to participate in further discussion, I complied, and fell into the deep plush of the recliner. I shot my legs straight under the coffee table, and listened to the lullaby played by the wind outside. I fought with myself, trying to forget, if only for a moment, about everything, but there was a delicate, intriguing, yet somehow familiar whiff floating around me—I couldn't classify its origin.

I was not sure how long Pete was gone, but when he finally came back with the beer, he sat on the couch, but not too far from me. He took a sip of the beer and put the glass on the table. He never used a glass before. The thought drifted through me without any significance. Pete picked up a perfumed tan envelope. So, that was it. I could smell its aroma then even from the distance. I know I have seen it before. Did he show it to me? It looks familiar. I could see writing on the top of the envelope. It was addressed, but from the angle I was sitting, all I distinguished were black hand-written letters against the soft pale beige of the paper.

"Joe, my son," said Pete, and I was entirely alert by then. "Let's leave all our arguments aside, if you can. I won't hold a grudge—I completely understand you. I know it's hard for you to imagine, but I once was much the same as you are. You might laugh when I tell you we are not much different. But it's true. Sooner or later, you will see."

"I'm sorry, Pete," I said, even though I wasn't ready to say it. Not yet.

"You don't have to be sorry. I know you are hurt." He paused and nervously shook the envelope. "I was waiting for the best moment. And I think this would be it. It's time. I didn't want to trouble you before—I was asked not to, actually—so I had to hold off until now."

He didn't want to bother me? Was asked not to? By whom? What the hell is he talking about? My thoughts spun around but I sat at a standstill, waiting for his next move.

"This," he slapped the envelope against his open palm, "is for you." Pete leaned forward and extended the envelope to me. "From Sally," he added.

But I could already see it. How could I not recognize her handwriting before, and the fine bouquet that accompanied all of her correspondence?

I jumped, hitting the low coffee table with both of my knees. Pete's glass of beer danced dangerously on one edge, and then settled back, sloshing only drops on the glossy top. I could care less, even if a whole barrel had hit the floor. I held the envelope, my eyes fixed on Sally's simple, but powerful letters.

"Is it really from Sally?" I asked the obvious, trying to ascertain that I wasn't dreaming. I didn't need an answer; I had it in my hands. This plain envelope was a fragile part of my life.

"She gave it to me the same night she arrived—" said Pete.

"Why?" I asked. "Why would she write a letter to me?"

"I didn't ask, Joe—"

"Why right after she came to visit you?"

"Joe." I heard his anxious search for air. "I didn't ask her. You know Sally. She wouldn't tell me anyway. I can—"

"Why didn't you give it to me earlier?" I cried.

"Joe, you have been here, what? Two days?" Pete checked his watch, and poked it with his finger. "Three now." He moved his eyes at me. "You were going crazy. Wait, what am I saying? Even now you are and, by the way, don't feel bad—it's not only you. That's why. I had to wait for the right moment."

"And this, what do you call it, 'right moment' is now?" I was furious. "That's perfect timing. Long after midnight, after the funeral, right after we returned from seeing my daughter who is lying in a coma. I don't know if she will ever wake up, and even if she does, if she is ever going to be the same."

"Nothing will ever be the same, Joe. Nothing." Pete's voice was sad, and he stopped hiding it. His voice sounded even lower than usual, and his slow pronunciation of words, made me peek at his tired face. I could see the grief of a father who had just lost his only daughter. How stupid was I, not to have seen that before? I was thinking only about myself, oblivious to the world outside. I grasped that Pete had been through something like this before—first, he lost his wife more than thirty years ago, and now Sally. My consternation mixed with horror and guilt. What kind of a dumb ass am I?

"I'm sorry, Pete." That was the only thing I could come up with. I was sure it wasn't nearly enough, so I tried to hug him.

"Never mind," he said, breaking the contact. "I know what you are going through." He paused. "Won't you read it?"

I checked the envelope again. I had identified Sally's handwriting before but only then could I see it was addressed to me. I fought the temptation to tear it open right away. I was so excited I couldn't wait, but, at the same time, I wasn't sure how to do it. My wife…Sally…a letter, she wrote it just before…

"Pete, do you mind if I read it alone first?" I said after a long pause.

"It's yours, Joe, not mine. Do what you think is best." He looked at me. "Go ahead."

I was already in the hallway, leaping up the steps. Opening the door to Sally's bedroom, I thought I heard Pete say something, but then nothing mattered. Even if he did, I wouldn't be able to comprehend anything anyway.

The soft light of the lamp by the bed was soothing. I placed the envelope on the bed and sat next to it, not daring to touch it, afraid and curious. Fascinated, my concentration glided away. How had that unpretentious little stationery taken over my whole world in a split second? Its delicate essence fluttered about the room in light waves, teasing my senses. When I had tamed my emotions enough to handle it, I touched the envelope as delicately as possible.

I treated it like a brittle gemstone that could be broken by just the shaking of my hands. I sat on the edge of the bed, holding something I never thought I would see. The letter carried her trace, an intoxicating spell that disarmed me thoroughly. I lost control of my thoughts; they meandered about, unaffected by reality. They beckoned me to stay in this safe shell forever. Just forget it all and let the whole world vanish. Without a doubt, it was a tempting idea. It would be such an easy choice for me, I thought, until I realized that I was being deceived by my own imagination.

It took a few minutes before I came back down to earth. The letter! I can't recall ever desiring anything so desperately, but even as it lay right there on my lap, I wasn't able to act. I craved her words, yet irrational fear kept me from sliding my finger under the flap and popping the envelope open. I pulled myself together, and wiped my palms over my wobbly legs.

Handling the treasure carefully, I opened the envelope, and took out a leaf of matching buff stationary. When I gently unfolded the page, I felt Sally's presence next to me, as if she sat waiting for me to begin reading. My heart knew it was true, but my mind couldn't accept it. I wrestled with the reality that I was holding her last letter, that it was her way of saying good-bye. Why? Her neatly inked letters sprung to my eyes so fast, I couldn't keep them organized.

> *Joe,*
>
> *I know how hard it must be for you to read these words but I beg you, I beg you, please read it carefully to the end. Even if you think that it doesn't make any sense at all, the only thing I ask you to do is to trust me. You have always trusted me through all our years together, so please trust me this last time. I must hurry, for I don't know when the inevitable will happen. All that I know is that it is going to happen very soon. I hope, no, I am sure, that Rosie will be fine. She will need a lot of help and attention, but she will be all right. As far as I'm concerned—well, don't worry about me. I'll manage. I'll be OK there, I know.*

I smiled through my tears; it was pure Sally. She couldn't be duplicated.

> *Whatever happens, no one will be able to explain. If you want to find out the truth, you are able to, but only if you really want to know. There is a truth out there for you to discover. All you have to do is reach out for it for yourself. That's why I beg you again. I beg you, and I hope you love me enough to make a trip for me and Rosie, most importantly for Rosie. This coming May, I want you to go to France. I know you'll find it very odd that my last request is for you to take a journey, but please trust me. Let's travel together. There is no other way. My father will prepare everything for you once you tell him what I*

have asked you to do. Remember, Joe, you can understand only if you really want to. But you have to do it on your own. You will meet a lot of people who are ready to help you, but everything is in your hands, remember that.

I love you and Rosie with all my heart. I'll see you again—trust me.

Sally

Chapter 4

The night's strangeness deepened with every passing hour. Effectively taken aback, my need for sleep slipped away in the face of my dismal reality. Alternately sitting on Sally's bed, and then pacing the length of her room, I thought about her letter. And the more I thought about it, the more uncertain I was about my beliefs. She knew. There is no question about that. I know she was aware that something was going to happen. But why? And what about Rosie? There were no easy answers waiting for me. And if there were any, they remained concealed from my sight. Slides from the past flashed through my mind like the huge neon signs on the side of a highway. I noticed them but drove by too quickly to grasp what they meant.

We had spent many wonderful years together, and I knew her well enough to have confidence in whatever she was doing or saying. I knew when she was serious, and when she was just fooling around. I also knew she would never do anything to put me in this position if she wasn't absolutely sure that would be for the best. She liked practical jokes; she loved to pull them on everybody, but this situation wasn't comical at all.

I learned her slowly, one small step at a time, and every new day with her had only convinced me how extraordinary she was. Was I able to comprehend all that she was giving me? I wasn't sure anymore. Long ago, I stopped wondering why so many people regarded her with such respect. Even if she was meeting them for the first time, she had an ineffable quality of capturing people's attention, and they seemed to appreciate her being upon that first greeting. She didn't have to say a word; yet somehow she was always at the center of conversation. Some would say just about everybody venerated her.

What was even more interesting, I couldn't recall a single person who didn't wish her well; most of the people I remembered were touched by her in some way. The more I thought about Sally that night, the closer I drew to the conclusion that maybe I didn't actually know who she truly was. I loved her as much as I possibly could, but like most men in love, I had been blinded by my own image of her. At last, I figured out that I didn't see her as she was, but only as I perceived her.

I thought I knew her well. The strangest part of this discovery was that, until tonight, I hadn't recognized how complicated and mysterious she was; I took her for granted. I didn't doubt she loved me—it was not about that. She did. I was sure—I felt that. It was something else. It was an inexplicable feeling that she had encompassed much more of humanity in her love than just our daughter and me. Her love was broader than this; in addition to us, she kept an open place in her heart for countless other people. In all the time we had spent together, she always poured abundant energy and compassion toward people in need. Her volunteer work in a variety of nonprofit organizations, which I had thought of as her "utopian whims," suddenly started to feel logical to me tonight. It hit me without warning—she had done all that because she honestly wanted to help. She really wanted to change the world with her own two hands.

How could I have missed all of that? Where had I been all those years that I hadn't clearly seen this side of her—that I didn't fully understand her actions? I was like a teenager who cut class, and a parent later caught me off guard and demanded an explanation.

I remembered how strangers looked at her. I hadn't paid attention at the time, but now—candles of hope lit up in their eyes. They loved her; they almost worshipped her. It was a very bizarre feeling, when tonight finally I became conscious of the fact that I didn't know my wife, my Sally, my real Sally, at all. I only thought I knew her. And what was worse, she had done everything possible to show me who she was. She hid nothing—it was all out in the open. I just didn't see it—it was me—I noticed only fragments of her. I never looked at Sally from the right angle, but approached her solely as a husband and a lover.

With the letter lying on my lap, which I had read dozens of times, I wasn't sure what to do. I felt obliged to obey her last wish. In fact, it never crossed my mind not to. Nevertheless, it seemed rather a strange request in any situation, doubly so in my present circumstances. Why France? Why in May? I thought, and the only logical explanation seemed to be that she wanted me to visit the country of her ancestors. She had mentioned once or twice that her family roots began in France, but nothing more than that. So what could possibly come from such an extraordinary request? It was yet another question I couldn't answer. And even if I considered taking that trip, I wasn't sure how to do it. How could I leave Rosemary here and just go away? How would I explain to her why I was gone when she woke up?

She is not going to wake up, face it.

I pushed that poisonous thought away before it could take root in my brain. She will. It's just a matter of time. It didn't sound convincing, and I knew it. I felt ashamed.

What about Pete? He knows something! I jumped. My first reaction was to wake him up, but I stopped at the door and turned back. I needed to assess everything before speaking with him. I suspected—no, I was sure—he was aware of something I wasn't. Something I had missed, or was never informed about—I didn't know which hurt more.

It looks kind of strange. If he knows something I have to get him to talk to me. He had to—Sally wrote that Pete would know what to do once I mention her request. But I also had no doubt that it wouldn't be easy to get him to divulge that information. I had to prepare. I had no clue what was going on, or what I was up against. I had no directions about where to start, or how to put the puzzle pieces together. I couldn't concentrate: late-night hours have never been my ally, and my thoughts jerked around in circles like an untamed horse. After hours of this fruitless speculation, my brain gave up, and with the first signs of the cold, crispy dawn, I fell into a shallow, jittery sleep.

When I woke up, I heard Pete already roaming around downstairs. I jumped off the bed, making sure the letter was intact and ran down the steps.

"You don't look so good," Pete observed.

"I know; I couldn't sleep," I replied.

"Me neither. I've been up all night," he said. "I could swear that I heard you moving about in the room. I almost knocked, but stopped—I wasn't sure how welcome I'd be."

"You should have come in." A strange feeling washed over me as I said that. "Maybe my head wouldn't be killing me."

Pete watched at me so closely I almost felt his scrutiny touching my face "Trust me, Joe, it will get better. I've been through it too." He paused. "Do you want some coffee? I made us a fresh pot."

No questions about the letter? That's strange. Why?

I drew in the delicious fragrance of fresh-brewed coffee, which I assumed, was supposed to make me feel better, but it fell short of its purpose. Sitting at the breakfast table with large mugs in our hands, we sipped hot, mild liquid silently, both focused on a point just beyond each other's back.

"Are you hungry?" Pete asked, setting his cup down.

"No, thanks. I think I'll skip breakfast today."

"You have to eat. Now you have to be strong." Pete's typically calm tone sounded slightly off key.

"Aren't you going to ask me about Sally's letter?" I couldn't resist.

"I was waiting for you to tell me. Do you want to talk about that?"

"I almost woke you up last night too," I said, my words tripping in haste. "You see I can't make anything out of her letter, her request...nothing... it's not logical, to be honest with you."

"You should have come; I wasn't sleeping anyway. I was thinking about all of them. You see my daughter—"

"Sally is asking me to go to France," I interrupted him. I didn't mean to, but it just flew out of my mouth.

"I know," said Pete after a long period of silence.

"How? How do you know?"

"You see...she...she told me so when she gave me that letter."

I wasn't sure why but it didn't sound like the whole story to me. Somehow I sensed that he is telling me only a half-truth, but in the last moment I changed my strategy, if I had any, deciding not to drill into this, at least right then.

"Why didn't you tell me earlier? Why didn't you give me this letter as soon as I arrived?" I said.

"I couldn't." Pete scratched his forehead. "Sally asked me to wait until—"

"What exactly did she say?" I cut in.

"To wait until the right moment."

"The 'right moment'?" I said. "What do you mean the 'right moment'?"

"That's exactly what she said."

"So how did you figure out when that was?"

"I didn't have to—it just happened by itself. I wanted to give it to you before the funeral, but with everything what was going on, with Rosie, and you… I saw what you were going through, and decided to wait."

"So," I asked, putting aside his explanations for the moment, "can you tell me how it is possible?"

"How what is possible?" Pete seemed to be a little embarrassed.

"How come Sally was able to write that kind of letter to me, like she—she knew she was going to die?"

"She did, Joe," said Pete, lowering his head. "Don't ask me why, but she knew it from the moment she arrived here. She didn't say much, but I noticed something…she acted like she was preparing, same as my—" Pete's voice cracked and I could see that it was too much for him. "Why don't you believe me? What reason would I have to not give that letter to you?"

"I don't know. Everything is so confusing. And also that—" I stopped short. I wanted to tell him about the weird incident last night in the woods, but something inside told me to be silent. I didn't know the reason, but instinctively felt it would be better if I kept it to myself.

"Also what?" Pete shifted in his chair.

"Nothing, I just got confused, that's all."

"If you want to know, I have a feeling that it's just the beginning," he said.

Here we go again. Once again, I couldn't understand why he would say such a thing. Was it a hint? If so, what the hell did it mean? He knows something I don't. I'm sure. Why is he not telling me everything?

"So, did you read the letter?" I asked straight out.

"No, but I know what it is about," Pete said calmly.

"So, you read it." I didn't see an alternative.

"No, I told you. I couldn't. It was addressed to you."

"So how would you know what's written there?"

"Joe, it's a long story. To keep it simple, I'll say that I was filled in on the details."

"Which is not true." I was dead serious.

"How could you, Joe?" Pete didn't seem to be as offended as he pretended to be. "It's all true."

"What do you think about that? What do you think about what Sally asked me to do?" I gave up. There was no point pursuing the issue of how he was familiar with the contents of the letter. I realized that our conversation would lead nowhere.

"Everything is up to you," he said, and covered his eyes with his beefy hand. "Whatever you do, it has to be your choice."

"So, you think I should leave everything and go to France?" I asked, staring straight at him. He didn't move his hand.

"I didn't say that. What I said was that everything is in your hands. Whatever you decide to do is your choice only."

"But Rosemary?" I couldn't even think about leaving her. "Even if I decide to go, what is going to happen to her?"

"I'll be here." It was short statement, but I knew Pete would stand behind it. He would probably spend every free minute in that hospital room.

"What am I going to tell her when she wakes up and finds I'm not there?" I paused. "What will happen if—if she doesn't wake up and—"

"Joe! She will wake up." Pete's hand slammed down on the table. "All you have to do is believe." His blazing eyes open, Pete's tone changed. "Don't you even think like that about Rosie."

"You're right, but I just can't stand being so helpless. There has to be something I can do—" I said, utterly at a loss.

"Trust in Sally," said Pete, calm once again. "Believe in her." A total peace encompassed the small kitchen; even the wind seemed to ease away from its constant humming. I sat, my thoughts wandering between two worlds, unsatisfied with Pete's answers, still without clear guidance, searching for the right solution. "Believe Sally," I heard Pete's voice. "If anything can help Rosie, it will come from your belief in Sally. That is the only way."

"OK, fine, let's pretend I decided to go." I said, perhaps with a little too much sarcasm. "I have to get back, first. Then, what about my job, our home? Rosie's school? They said they could move Rosie to…What about money? We…I don't have that much cash. In truth, my savings are nearly drowned."

"Joe, all you can see are the problems," Pete's voice began to work on me. I accepted it, admitted, and surrendered, being unable to stand against his iron will. "First of all, you know Rosie is going to stay here. They won't transfer her to any other hospital, not until they are one hundred percent sure what is wrong with her. And even then, she might end up staying here anyway."

"You're right," I said.

"You know I will take good care of her."

"I know, Pete, I know."

"So, your problem is not how to go back to New York, but how to move here."

"But my job and the house—" I was shocked by the way he just decided what would be best for me, for us, but deep in my heart, I agreed; he was right. I should move here, whether I decided to heed the Sally's request or not. I couldn't live in Greenpoint, knowing that my daughter was here, knowing that I couldn't see her every day.

"As far as I know, you are renting that house," Pete continued without waiting for an answer. "When is your lease up?"

I thought for a minute. "By the end of August, I think."

"You have to check it out, just to be sure. For now, let's see…did you pay your rent this month?"

"Yes."

"So, it leaves us with what?" Pete counted the months on his fingers. "Seven months of payments?"

"I think I know where you're going with this, but I don't have that much money."

He didn't listen to me. "I assume…I'm sure that you put up the security deposit."

"Two months."

"So…" Again he used his fingers. "We would have to come up with five months of rent in case the landlord won't let you out of the lease early."

"He won't. I know him." And I really knew the guy. One of those sleazy types—middle-aged and overweight man with low-priced vodka running through his veins, who acted like he owned not only the building, but also the tenants themselves. He never did any repairs, blamed everyone else for destroying his property, and constantly tried to raise the rent.

"He's a complete jerk. He'll probably ask for all seven months plus the security deposit for damages he supposedly incurred. And anyway, even if for some strange reason he settles for five, I still won't have enough money for a trip to France or Rosie's medical bills."

"But you haven't tried to ask him yet, have you?" said Pete.

"Of course not. I am here, and we...you...just came up with this idea, or plan, if it could even be called a 'plan,'" I said. I was certain that, whatever Pete was up to, the part with the landlord wasn't workable at all. "Pete, where are you going with this?"

"Where?" Pete's face brightened. "Isn't it clear? What I am suggesting is for you to move here with me and then take it from there. There will be plenty of time for you to think about the..." It seemed like he was searching for the right word. "Everything."

"Maybe you're right," I said, unconvinced. "But what about my job? I can't stop working now, especially if I decide to go. I need money, not only for that, for Rosie too. I could probably ask my parents for some help, but—"

"There is plenty of work for good carpenters," Pete cut in. "Well, I can say that I know most of the people in the village. There are very few homes I haven't worked on around here. Everyone knows me. I'll get you hooked up in no time."

"Pete, are you serious? I can't let you take all of this on your shoulders."

"You and Rosie are the only family I have left. I want you to understand that." He paused. "I need you here."

I didn't say anything for a while, glancing at the pictures of Sally and Rosie that hung on the walls. They looked like sisters, the same smiling eyes, the same red hair, the same expression, and the same body language. There was something magical in those photos, something I couldn't name. Then right next to their pictures hung another photo. It was the one that captivated my attention. At first, I thought it was Sally, then Rosie, but I couldn't decide who had been captured in this monochrome photo.

"You never met her, did you?" I heard Pete. "Of course— you couldn't. It's Maggie, my wife."

"Oh, I think I've seen her picture before." I said. "She looks just like—"

"They all look alike." Pete laughed. "You should have seen my reaction when I saw Maggie's mother for the first time. I thought it was her twin sister."

"That's what I thought; if not for the age difference, I would say they were triplets."

"I think of it as pictures of one person in different stages of life."

"It's unbelievable."

"I agree," said Pete. "Everything is unbelievable." He leaned back in his chair.

I sipped some more of the cold coffee, gauging his response to my next words.

"Hm…Pete, everything sounds great. I move here, you find work for me, but what about the money? Even if I decide to go, I won't able to make enough even to pay for the tickets."

"Don't worry about that now. You still have a few months, we'll manage somehow. It was Sally's last wish and I'll do everything I can to make sure it's fulfilled. For now, just take care of the house and come back here. And if the landlord gives you any problems," his face darkened, "call me, and I'll talk to him." He paused. "Come back as soon as you can. I'm going to have a job waiting for you."

"It's not as easy as it sounds," I said, but Pete wasn't listening.

"How long do you need? A few days?"

"More like a week. I'll have to sort our stuff and decide what to bring here," I said without hesitation. I couldn't understand why I had said that. I wasn't sure yet if that was exactly what I intended to do. It seemed that my whole life had begun to stream ahead without even minimal participation from my side. My consent was not necessary to put everything in motion—the decisions had been already made. And I honestly thought I started to like it that way.

"Very well, then." I could see that Pete's thoughts had moved on to something else already. "Let's go see Rosie, and then off you go. You have a plane to catch."

I looked at him skeptically, but he had already turned his back to me, leaving me sitting at the table alone.

Chapter 5

Greenpoint, an antiquated neighborhood of New York City, greeted me with the unforgettable vapor of overcooked cabbage and endless laundry, topped with a slight touch of gasoline fumes. This unique tang had accompanied this place as far back as I could remember. Its roots ran so deep; everybody either moved out or accepted it as it was. Sometimes it seemed the stench abated, and for a couple of days people learned how to breathe fresh air again. But in the end, it always came back, more determined than ever to embrace the area in its grimy arms.

I had lived here all my life. My parents moved out right after I was old enough to make it on my own. Later, to my astonishment, I decided to stay, just because it seemed the right thing to do. As a child, I ran the dangerous streets, seeking adventure in the vacant buildings scattered through the neighborhood. I couldn't just leave those memories behind. I learned my ABCs by reading the street names south of Manhattan Avenue. I trained my slingshot skills by hunting rats with my friends. I tasted first kisses and not-so-innocent touches in the shadows of the derelict movie theater's marquee. I remembered everything clearly, but this time the picture was slightly askew. Even if it wasn't as vivid and colorful as I'd thought, I felt like I was committing adultery as I made the final decision to move to Fox River Valley Gardens with Pete. All at once I became aware of how much I was going to miss this tainted place.

The small apartment building stood amid the cluster of box-like units, its aluminum siding a sickly depressing sight. Wrought iron fence extended along the property, supposedly for our protection, was little more than a poor decoration. But Sally and I liked that place. We lived here for almost eight years, since just before Rosie was born. We had never talked about moving out. We'd simply nestled into its extraordinary charm and accepted its faults without question.

Sally loved Greenpoint. For people here, principles were simple: survive with all the dignity you could muster, and live an honest life. She quickly accepted the fact she couldn't communicate with the neighbors, for the most of the time. I barely could. My parents never taught me to speak Polish. We used broken English at home. They tried so hard to "Americanize" not only their speech, but also their manners that it became funny. But they didn't see the damage that such neglect to our family would cost. If not for my childish contrariness, I might have missed out on so many tasty things in those small ethnic stores I frequented. I would never have been aware of my customs.

I loved our neighborhood, my friends, and, in spite of my parents' disapproval, I felt like I was one of them. Now that I was about to leave it, I was betraying our tradition, our heritage. Moreover, everything good that had happened in my life was somehow connected to this small inconsequential piece of earth.

It was here that I first met Sally. She was helping to organize a fundraising event in our neighborhood for the Red Cross. Her decision surprised me, and I wondered if the choice was carefully planned or purely accidental. The whole idea seemed like a lost cause, since we were more likely to be the recipients than donors, but Sally proved me wrong, and not for the last time.

I remember as if it was yesterday. Dressed in blue jeans and a white T-shirt with a Red Cross logo, she stood by the table sorting and filling out papers, her auburn hair pulled back in a ponytail. Even though her complexion wasn't causing too much interest on the street, her smooth olive skin distinguished her from the crowd. At first, I just passed her by, but after few steps, I stopped and came back not far from the table. I could see her, but tried to keep a safe distance so I would remain unnoticed. And I spied on her. By the time the fundraising activities ended, the sun was setting. I saw her folding tables and chairs, and realized that she was about to leave. I gathered all the courage inside of me and approached her, though the patchy pavement seemed to quiver beneath my feet.

"Finally," she said before I could speak.

"Finally?" My knees hardly supported the weight of my body.

"I saw you watching me all afternoon." She smiled, pointing in the direction where I had been standing.

"I'm sorry. I didn't mean to—"

"You didn't mean? Too bad." She was still smiling. The other volunteers continued to close out the stands, exchanging smiles and stifling snickers. Sally paid no attention to them.

"So I'll have to leave, I guess." She turned away.

"No, wait. Please." My words tumbled out a little too loudly.

"Yes?" She stopped and turned back. The only thing I saw was her coffee-colored eyes. They filled my whole world.

"Would you...would...I...Can you stay with me...for a while?"

I didn't exactly know what I was saying, but the result of my incompetent bungling was unexpected and miraculous. We had remained together since that day. Until—.

I didn't think I could bear it. Walking into our apartment, I was filled with a barrage of emotions. Nobody can replace all those little things that were said or done here. I felt her presence every-where. Then Rosie was born, and those moments with her were playful, cheerful times, free of worries. Nothing was more important than the fact we had been together. I tightened my grip on myself, but I couldn't hold it in. I knew then—nothing would be the same anymore.

It took me a couple of days—hours spent daydreaming, re-membering—until I was ready to go on. I didn't adjust to the thought that she was no longer with me. I just eased myself into a numb state of delusion. I managed to speak with Pete at least twice a day to check on Rosie's condition. As the doctors expected, her prognosis hadn't changed.

I didn't go to work. I called my supervisor, Waldi. Knowing his everyday habits, I chose the best time to ensure my call would go directly to his voice mail, and I left him a short message. I wasn't ready to deal with pity, and all those fretful stares I was sure to receive from my buddies. I didn't call them, hoping they would understand. In a way, they probably appreciated it. No group therapy was necessary; I'd had enough of it already.

It was late morning when someone knocked. Automatically I opened the door.

"Listen, Joe, I can't imagine how hard it is for you. I don't have a darn idea—" Andy was the owner of the company, a good man, an older immigrant whose life was limited to his construction projects. He came in without invitation.

"Nobody does," I said.

"You're right, Joe." He paused. "I know you have to leave—"

"I just called Waldi," I said. "I left him a message."

"I know, I know. That's why I am here." He searched for something, patting his jacket pockets. "Here is your last check."

"What?" I said. "I didn't work for the last couple of weeks. I don't think you owe me anything."

"Oh, come on, Joe. I know better. Here it is."

"Andy," I said, trying hard not to lower my eyes to the check. "You know I'm not coming back. Don't you?"

"I know, I get it. We all do. We are so—"

"Andy, please stop it."

"OK, OK, I just can't—"

"Andy."

"OK," he said again. "I'm going, but before I go—" He searched his pockets again. "I have something for you." He seemed uncertain what else to say next after he took out a plain thick envelope.

"It wasn't necessary." I said, a little embarrassed, convinced of what I was going to find inside.

"No, Joe. It was. It's from us," he said. "From the boys, my wife and me, we know you're going to need it." He handed me the envelope.

I opened it up, and peeked inside.

"But, Andy, that's a lot of money. You shouldn't have."

"We thought it over." He wasn't about to discuss that matter. The decision had been made. "That's the least we can do for you," he said. "Everyone is going to miss you."

"I don't know what to say." I knew that I was going to miss them too. Maybe not all of them; some of the characters I had to work with weren't my favorites, but I'd miss Andy and his wife for sure.

"You don't have to say anything." He moved toward the door. "I have to go, before—"

"Thank you," I said, as he paused outside the door. "Thank all of them for me, please."

"I will." We shook hands. "Take care, boy, and remember— if you need help, you just come straight to me. Don't hesitate."

"Thanks, Andy," I said. "I'll remember that."

I had an odd feeling when he left. I thought about how most people reacted when faced with tragedy, especially if it didn't touch them directly. The toughest ones became unsure of themselves, and those who had never shown initiative suddenly became leaders. I liked Andy; I couldn't say one bad word about him. He and his wife had always treated Sally and I like family, so I could easily forgive his blundering efforts at tact and sympathy. I was grateful for the gift. It was so unexpected I didn't admit it had happened until I opened the envelope again. They didn't know and they could never imagine how much I was going to need it.

Not everything came that easily. The shadow of the landlord circled like a vulture awaiting its turn. I spoke to him two or three times during my lethargy, but I didn't remember much of what was said, aside from threats of lawsuit if I didn't pay the remainder of the lease. I was the last person to declare it, but I didn't really blame him. Nevertheless, I wasn't too eager to comply. But simply, I didn't have any other option available. I slowly counted the money and placed it on the kitchen table. With this, and the measly change I have in the bank, I thought, I will still have some money left after paying him off.

I didn't have to pay him off. It would be so easy just to move out, and forget about him. He wouldn't be able do anything to me if he couldn't find me. If not for Sally, I might have considered that option, but this wasn't my way anymore. Since I met her, Sally showed me many things I didn't know, or maybe I hadn't seen before. Many little things were so dissimilar from the world's accepted standards that sometimes I wondered, where did she come from? She was too good and too generous; I thought she must have come from a different world.

I delayed my return to our bedroom as long as possible. I sat by the kitchen table sipping coffee—yesterday's or the day's before—trying to forget about everything that had happened recently. The chair was comfortable enough for me to observe the snowy window until it turned bleak. It became darker and darker with every minute, until it was only a funereal rectangular on the wall, staring inside the apartment at me. I shut the blinds to make it disappear, but I knew it didn't help. My subconscious wasn't that easy to cheat.

I went back to the bedroom with every intention of packing. And I tried. A few belongings lay spread around, waiting to be boxed up. I decided to leave most of our stuff behind, giving the majority to charity, and taking only the most essential necessities. I was tempted to leave everything outright, and never reclaim it. Too much of our life rested in each item, but I didn't think Sally would approve. If the situation were reversed, I knew she wouldn't try to dispose of our reflections from the past. So, with my heart deliberately mangled by the jaws of memories, I filled up the carton coffins little by little. Rosie's room was contained in two or three boxes, not counting her toys. They would require a separate truck to carry them off, and I wasn't even sure one vehicle would be enough. Mine didn't take too much space, either. I was amused by how uncomplicated our life had been until the accident.

When it came to Sally's personal effects, I broke down. I understood I had to do it, but I wasn't ready yet. I lay down on our bed and closed my eyes, hoping something would happen to spare me this duty. Nothing happened. I knew too well it wouldn't. I was only delaying the inevitable rather than facing the chore I would eventually have to do.

I kept only her most cherished possessions, nothing else; her pictures, a few dresses that we had both liked and that comforted me to hold near, and the meager pieces of jewelry. She never wore such trinkets. She liked them, I supposed, but if asked, I couldn't recall when I'd last seen her wearing a necklace, or a ring, or even her wedding band.

The remnants of what we used to call our home lay scattered around the apartment, ready for the Red Cross to pick up. They were coming later in the evening, and I hoped the driver was going to bring extra help. I knew that I was not coming back here, not to the apartment, not even to the neighborhood. Anywhere— but here.

When I was done, I was no longer afraid to open the blinds in the kitchen again—the black hole wasn't staring inside anymore. But it wasn't gone; it just got replaced by the empty translucent box. I went back to the bedroom, sat on our naked bed, and inspected the bare walls and furniture no longer ours. Boxes I would take with me filled Rosie's bedroom. For the hundredth time, my eyes raked the room when the clock on the nightstand halted my inspection. It wasn't the clock itself; I had decided to leave it. I caught a glimpse of something I'd missed behind the clock. I leaned forward and grabbed the shiny frame. A flush of guilt washed over me. How could I have missed that? I hadn't seen that picture of our family for a long time. When I didn't see it anywhere, I assumed Sally must have taken it with her. It was taken in one of the happiest moments of our life, on a warm Sunday evening by the Hudson River, with all the lights of New York glowing in the background; three untroubled smiling faces with halos. With hesitant hands, I placed our picture inside my pocket.

Loud knocking rescued me before my mind went spinning again.

"Come on in. The door is open," I shouted. "I am in the bedroom." I thought it was the Red Cross crew. Scared by my exaggerated description of the volume of goods they were supposed to pick up, maybe they had arrived early. Instead, someone I did not anticipate, entered the apartment.

It was my landlord.

Oh, shit. I forgot to call him yesterday, and now he came to bust my balls. Great!

I invited him into the kitchen, trying to delay one of his legendary outbursts, which was surely waiting for its moment of glory. We settled by the table where the envelope full of bills was in plain sight; I wouldn't be able to hide it now, even if I wanted.

"Joe, before you say anything, hear me out, please," he said.

His English reminded me of the dialect of my parents.

He must know. I judged it by how he pronounced each word carefully. Have I told him? No, it wasn't me. I was sure he didn't hear anything from me, but it was obvious he knew.

"Don't worry, I have your money." I said, as amiably as I could under the circumstances, and I reached for the envelope. "I have to cut you a check for the difference, if that's OK with you?"

He raised his hands, and waved them in the air. "Oh, no, no. That's not what I am here for."

"What else might you want from me?" My guard was up immediately. "I don't think we have anything else to discuss."

"I am sorry, Joe. I came to apologize," he said.

"What?"

"Listen, Joe, I have to admit, I acted like a total jerk," he said, pulling something out of his puffy jacket pocket. His hand flew straight up in my direction. "Please understand. Please." He unfolded a piece of paper. "Here is a check for your security deposit, the whole amount. Now we are even, and don't worry about anything else. I really just came to apologize to you."

His words sounded like a record played in fast-forward. I heard what was he saying yet I couldn't comprehend it. Before I made out what had just happened, he was gone. I was alone in the kitchen with the envelope of cash in one hand, and the landlord's check in my other one. I wasn't sure if this was just a daydream, or if someone was playing sick jokes on me. I poked myself. It hurt. Avoiding further contemplation, I began carrying boxes out of the Rosie's bedroom, and hauled them to my truck.

Chapter 6

The last ten years of my life had been stuffed inside a few cardboard boxes, a mosaic of memories filling our Ford Explorer to the roof. I had to admit to myself that I would never be able to get anything back, but I couldn't care less. Nothing mattered now—nothing except Rosie. She was the only person I, in truth, cared for, and I felt as if a bullet pierced my skull every time I contemplated what lay ahead for her, for me, for both of us. I was trying to grasp one straightforward rule—for the rest of my life I was going to have to live with whatever the future held, I had no control over anything. I was afraid of how I would cope with that. I didn't want to be a pessimist, but I couldn't keep myself from visualizing yet another silent and gloomy event in my life—

Rosie, wearing a white dress to offset her red hair, smiling, yet lying calmly in a glossy pearl casket.

This vivid, lifelike image stayed hidden most of the time in the clouded recesses of my battered psyche, but periodically, it popped up like an unwanted window on a computer screen. I just couldn't close it down. It kept returning uninvited. The thought always brought the most gruesome, horrible feeling of depression I had ever faced. I would trade my own soul to make it vanish. But that was impossible because Rosie's death was something I feared the most.

I was vulnerable, unprepared, and too weak to fight the battle I was going to lose anyway. Everything I'd touched so far, everything I'd ever loved dissolved already, or was slowly melting away. I had to develop some kind of safety net that would allow me to function in this hopeless, drab world. The only problem was that I didn't have a recipe for accomplishing this task. Altogether, with that sixteen-hour or so drive ahead of me, there was nothing to look forward to. Accompanied by the time's bleeding stings, the road before me coiled into points unknown, and I could find no one to help me.

During my ride back to Fox River Valley Gardens, I called Pete and the hospital every few hours, even into the night. The answer was the same over and over again—no change. I was close to the point where I would stop believing that I was ever going to hear anything else but that chilly slogan. I was terrified that deep inside, part of me was almost ready to accept this situation, to accept and embrace this madness. But planted by Sally's last words, hidden away in my heart, invisible and undetectable, there was an irrational seed of hope, tiny and shy, but indestructible and insepa-rable from myself. And this, above all else, carried me on. Even if I wasn't sure how to feel about it, it was there, and it had been the only source of power that kept me going.

I tried not to think while driving, just concentrate on the road, but it seemed impossible. Every time I found myself alone, with no car lights around to keep me company, my mind shifted into playback mode. Taking advantage of the dull monotony of a half-empty highway, panoramic slides played against my windshield. Those wounding scenes couldn't have picked a better moment to torture me. Their timing was perfect. Unsure, afraid, each waiting for the other to make the first move, we lay down, curled up in the warmth of the night. Embraced by the fascinating touch of the unknown, I desired her, affection paralyzing my every move. She was next to me, her olive skin waiting to be touched…I was so happy…

When I woke up the next morning, I sat on the bed, careful not to wake her up, striving to memorize everything about her. Her long, loose hair—more red than brown—spread on the pillow and blanketed half of her face. Her arms contrasted with the pastiness of the quilt, and her slim fingers folded slightly, as if resting on the ivories of an imaginary piano. The lovely freckle between the thumb and the index finger was visible on her right hand. She seemed so vulnerable. She was close, yet I was afraid to touch her, as if she would dematerialize at the contact. I couldn't stop wondering why she had chosen me. Not because it bothered me—I felt lucky—but her enigmatic decision made me a little nervous. I didn't want to lose her, and had already become a little jealous. Sally could have any man on the planet and I was sure he would jump up and down at her nod. Yet she picked a pathetic high school graduate carpenter. I was both happy and afraid at the same time. Afraid that this was some kind of a game for her, a little play she wanted to tease me with; when she'd had enough of me, she would just toss the toy aside.

As if she was able to read my thoughts, Sally opened her eyes and smiled. She pulled toward me and placed her head on my lap, wrapping her arm around me. "I love to play with my toys for a very long time," she said after a while. "I don't toss them away that easily. If fact, I never throw anything away, Joe. Are you ready for this?"

I didn't know what to say. Struggling to find the right words, I sat there like a dummy.

"I love you," she said with a smile, squeezing me in her arms.

I had to stop. I couldn't breathe. Her hug had cut off my air. I pulled over to the side of the road, and parked in the gravel. Cars honked loudly as they sped by. I didn't pay any attention. I just jumped out of my truck and ran through the snow.

Chapter 7

I arrived in Fox River Valley Gardens just before the dawn, after a protracted couple of hours spent in horrible traffic on the expressway on Chicago's South Side. I handled the driving rather well, but the constant fight with my own imagination exhausted me. On the wide screen of the Windshield Theatre, my whole life replayed in slow motion, with reruns of the best and worst moments. Even spectators with limitless patience would have fled. I was the only one who had to watch it, and worse, I had to stay to the end—I didn't have any other option.

The lights winking between the slats of the blinds had no chance against the evening's frosty dimness. I pulled my truck between the white mountains of snow on both sides of Pete's driveway. I felt a surge of relief. I was glad I had decided to move in with him, and I was thankful for his desire to help. He wasn't obligated to help me, and it would have been understandable. We never got to know each other well. But since our first meeting, just before the wedding, I found him to be a very intriguing person. After the first couple of visits, I discovered only a few similarities between us. But it wasn't until I stood in front of his home that chilly night, with my whole life in my truck, that I realized we were just alike.

Sally's mom, Maggie, also died early, leaving him with their only child. Pete had to sacrifice nearly everything to raise Sally. He used to own a construction company. From what I'd heard, he pulled such long hours to keep it up and running, he barely spent any time with his family. It wasn't true that he made tons of money that way. He was the type of person that satisfied the client, even if he had to do the job twice, and spend more than he was about to earn, if necessary. The old-school style. There were not too many like him around—an analog man. To keep a word once promised was worth more to him than all the money in his pocket. Some people—most of his customers, I suspected—took advantage of his business approach, and squeezed everything possible out of him, just because they could.

After Maggie's abrupt departure, he decided to sell the business and found work that gave him some stability, regular hours, and a decent paycheck, free of customer demands, so he could be with Sally. Pete had never remarried, and I didn't blame him for that. I've seen the similarity between Sally and Maggie in pictures, but if the two were as alike as people were saying—in their gestures, their touches, their beings—then I didn't blame him for that at all. Somehow, I sensed it already—I won't marry anyone else; I won't be looking. I couldn't, even though it might seem silly and eccentric to some people. They might even say it was a premature vow of a mourning spouse, but I was sure in my heart. Another woman was out of the question.

My own family had its share of oddities, but I was just beginning to learn how weird Sally's heritage was. If Maggie and her daughter were the same, Sally and Rosemary were identical. If not for age, it would be impossible to distinguish one from the other; they were exact copies. They didn't appear to be mother and daughter, more like sisters with vast differences in the birth date. I have also heard that Maggie was the reincarnation of her mother, Sally's grandmother, Mary-Ann. When Sally told me that, I laughed—until we visited her grandmother's grave.

One late summer afternoon, we took a trip to McHenry, where they used to live. Maggie and Mary-Ann were buried there in the same cemetery. We went to Sally's mom's site first. Located in the middle of the cemetery, the plain grave with a massive unevenly worn marble had settled on the ground. A large solitary candle was burning in front of the grave, lighting up its bright, coarse surface. I found it a little bit strange, but didn't say anything. I didn't want to hurt Sally's feelings. There was an old, pale picture of a woman approximately our age, attached to the stone. If Sally had not been standing next to me, I could swear it was hers. I even took hold of her hand the moment I laid eyes on the picture. It was the first time I grasped how close they truly were. I couldn't stop staring at Sally and the picture of her mom, but that wasn't the only shock. We walked to her grandmother's resting place. Again, it was a single, rough boulder placed over the site, and a nearly burned out candle. Another black and white picture of Sally suspiciously observed me from behind the weather-beaten glass cover. It was the same woman—Sally, or her mom, or her grandmother. I didn't know who that was. I was thankful Sally's great-grandmother wasn't buried here. I wasn't sure I could take it.

"I told you, Joe. It's been like that forever," said Sally. "You didn't want to believe me."

"It's not that—" I said. "It's just…just—"

"There is always a girl, and—"

"Oh, no, no, honey," I said. "Things can change. I can even agree he will have your looks. But it will be a him."

"There are no exceptions," said Sally softly. "Not one."

"Don't worry, honey," I said as I laughed. "Remember there are only a few girls on my side of the family, as far back as I remember. My mind rests easy."

I was so sure we would have a son it was beyond any questions. I just knew it. That indescribable certainty that things will happen according to plan had never let me down before. When Sally said she was pregnant, I was so proud, and so certain we would have a son that I didn't listen to her quiet words. She tried to explain, to prepare me for a different scenario. In my imagination, I played football games with my son, already throwing the ball high and far away, as my future wide receiver ran through the field for a touchdown.

Until, of course, the night when Rosemary was born.

Shocked, I suffered a quick moment of consternation. Then I accepted the situation as it was, and never complained about having two Sallies at home. We never had another conversation about the gender of our offspring.

I snapped out of yet another mental game just in time to park the tired, dirty truck beside the garage. Through the gusty cover, which attacked me as soon as I stepped out, I made it to the front. The door was unlocked, so I went right in. Pete was sitting in the kitchen with his elbows on the table, his head sagging above the newspaper. I couldn't see from that distance, but I had a feeling he was asleep. He dozed, but not deeply enough to let me pass by.

"Joe," he said, lifting his head slowly. "You're back."

"I'm sorry I didn't give you a heads-up. I got caught in bad traffic, and didn't think of it. Just tried to get out of the snow."

"That's not a problem. I know," he said. "I watched the evening news. It wasn't pretty out there—you must be tired."

"No question about that. It was quite an experience."

"Hungry?"

"Not at all. I haven't really eaten since—" I blinked as I realized I hadn't eaten a real meal in at least a week. Nothing but light snacks. "I completely forgot about food, Pete. And what's strange is that I am not hungry, not a bit."

"Well then, go to bed. We will take care of your stuff in the morning."

"I thought I would go see Rosemary," I said. "I'll just take a quick shower. Are you going with me?"

"I was there three or four times today." Pete's eyes met mine. "Nothing has changed."

"I just want to see her."

"Well, let's go, then."

Chapter 8

I found Rosie in the same condition she was in before I left for New York—silent and unresponsive. Nothing had changed—this mantra had been played once again. Realistically, I didn't expect any change overnight—I had spoken with Pete the night before I left Greenpoint, and then a few times on the road. But the feeling that something unexpected and miraculous could happen when I wasn't there was more powerful than logic. In my case, logic didn't work.

First of all, I couldn't fathom an explanation as to why such an incident had happened. At the same time, I couldn't shake the unexplainable feeling that there was something more to it, something I couldn't yet see. Something hidden beneath the surface of this tragedy in which I played only a supporting role. Everything was so blurred, so confusing, it was beyond my ability to understand. Everything except Rosie. When I stared at her fragile beauty, I was ready to offer all that I had, and more, to bring her back. I could lie, cheat, or commit the worst of sins if only it would help my daughter. I held her tiny hand, trying not to see the machinery coldly multiplying behind her. But this depressing equipment was the only sign she was still with us, that she hadn't left this world. In my devastated mind, I wished I could become an integral part of that gear and, by touching her, I might commence life into her.

I wasn't sad anymore; my sadness had changed to resignation. My consciousness told me that she in reality was gone, and I was not capable of doing anything to help her. I was powerless. It was beyond me; I couldn't make her come back. Sitting next to her, I conceded I had almost given up hope.

Hope—a feeling that was an integral part of Sally—she used it on a daily basis. Now I knew. She had tried to teach not only me, but also everyone she met, how important faith should be in our lives. I always treated her preaching with mild skepticism, but she never gave up. She always hoped that one day I would be able to value. And, for the first time in her life, apparently, she was wrong—it was beyond my comprehension.

"She'll be OK." Pete's voice broke through the humming silence. I wasn't sure how long I had been sitting by Rosie's bed, and felt uneasy that I had forgotten his presence.

"I wish I could be so sure," I said. I sensed his frown.

"You just have to have confidence in God," he said, taking a lungful of air.

"Pete, I don't want to get into this dispute with you. You know better. Let's leave God out of it." I didn't want to argue with him, especially in front of my daughter.

"Of course, Joe." He observed me closely. "I said that just because Sally would say the same thing if she were here."

"But she is not—" I was just about to scream. "And you know why?" I didn't let him answer. "Because…because your—"

"Joe, Joe." Pete grabbed my arm. "Stop that right now." He waited for me to calm down. "Just think for a moment. Think about Sally. You knew her better than anybody else."

That's only what you think, I almost said.

"What would she do?" He let go of my arm and stepped back. "What would she do, Joe?"

I had to agree—he'd made his point. If Sally were there, she would say exactly the same thing. She was the only person I met who trusted God's will and wisdom so much. I hadn't thought of that before. I just took everything as it was, and it never even occurred to me to question her.

"Pete, if you know more than you are telling me, I beg you to tell me right now." I didn't know what I was hoping for.

"I've already told you. I've told you everything—the doctors are very careful in their prognosis. But there is one more thing I will tell you over and over again, the same thing Sally would tell you if she was standing here right now. Have faith," he said and left the room.

I was perfectly aware of that , at least I thought I understood what was he saying. But it was one thing to comprehend something, and totally different to implement it. My whole life, I've had problems with the latter. Is he telling me the whole story, or is it my imagination? I thought as we left Rosie's room. Should I ask him straight out? Should I demand an explanation about Sally's letter and her request? What about this drunken Brad, or whoever, or whatever that was in the woods? Should I tell him?

There is a truth out there for you to discover…all you have to do is reach out for it for yourself…remember, Joe, you can understand only if you really want to…but everything is in your hands, remember that…Whatever happens, no one will be able to explain. I could swear I heard Sally's voice, but when I looked around there was no one else except Rosie and me around.

Chapter 9

The next morning my nightmare began rather than ended with the dawn. Reality hit me with a headache like a continuous drum roll. It was well before six when I crawled downstairs in search of painkillers, anything what would stop that horrible beating. The hoary quilt of forgetfulness covered the world outside, but thanks to the street lamp shining in the windows, I was able to find my way around without turning on the lights. I remembered that Pete kept some of his over-the-counter medications in the drawer of one of the small pantry cabinets. The problem was I didn't know exactly which drawer, and neither was I sure that I would find what I was attempting to find. So even before I started searching, I went through the tedious task of pouring water and four scoops of coffee into the coffee maker on the kitchen countertop, just in case. I've heard that strong coffee with lemon does as well as any painkiller, if not better. I had never tried that recipe before, but some of my buddies said it worked pretty well, especially after a long night out. I felt like I had been drinking for a week.

I didn't find a lemon in Pete's refrigerator, but there was one old, discolored lime. Deciding that it had to do, I cut a thick slice of the overripe fruit and laid it down next to the cup. The sour juice flowing from the lime made my hands sticky, and I wiped them on a paper towel. The noise of running water filling the coffee pot had been painful enough to make me think about stopping at once.

I was trying hard not to wake Pete up. Carefully, as silently as possible for a man in my condition, I went to the pantry. I rummaged through all the cabinets one by one in a fruitless search for a salutary pill to soothe the exploding shells in my head. I would kill for anything, even the smallest dose of acetaminophen, but I couldn't even find an aspirin, nothing except a few prescription medicines. But I had no idea of their purpose. I just browsed through them, noticing the names of drugs unknown to me, and put them back.

One more drawer remained not inspected. In desperation, but without much hope, I pulled it open. At first glance, it was just another drawer full of old papers. But somehow, my hand dug deep, as if by instinct. I wasn't sure what I was doing or why, but I took out all of the drawer's contents and placed them on the kitchen table.

I never thought of myself as a person who would go through someone else's possessions without permission. But the pile of yellowed pages cut from newspapers appeared so innocent that I allowed myself to look through them. There were more than enough flimsy reasons to justify my resolution: I didn't find any painkillers, my coffee was ready, and I didn't have anything better to do. A grayish piece of lime floated in the brackish liquid in my mug. I sat by the table and leaned against the window. It was bright enough to see clearly. Separate pages stuck to each other with the glue of time; I had to be very careful not to tear them when I began peeling them apart one by one.

It was quite a compilation gathered by Pete, or maybe even Maggie, throughout the years. It consisted of pages from newspapers, magazines, and a few childish hand drawings of a face I didn't recognize. Some were just plain empty pages torn from a notebook. Sipping the sour, but rejuvenating fluid, I sifted through those parched pages one by one, keeping them in the same order. After a while, tired of the repetition of picking up each page and placing it face down, I was ready to collect those two piles of papers in front of me, and put them back into the drawer. I checked the next in the stack, a clipping from a newspaper, and decided to give it one last chance. I tried to detach it undamaged from the pile, and, after a struggle, I unfolded it on the table, moving both stacks to the side.

It was hard to guess what newspaper it was from. The header was unreadable with the passage of time. In the middle, there was a large photograph. It was also faded, but visible enough to let the part of my brain unaffected by the headache catch a trace of significance. The blurry picture was part of an article that the newspaper published, but the article itself was missing. It seemed like the print dissolved over time, and only single letters, or partial words were speckled around the image. Only the title remained impervious, printed in bold letters, now washed out to light gray, just above the picture. I read it again: Mysterious farewell to a local volunteer.

I tried to find a date, but it wasn't visible at all. I finally took the page and spread it on the window pane. Only when the light penetrated the porous paper, was I able to decipher just a portion of the date. The newspaper was printed sometime in February of 1966.

I looked at the picture again. All I could make out was the smeared image of people holding candles. I could hardly see it; nevertheless, I was sure what I saw. One large candle soared over the small ones. I didn't have the slightest idea as to why I couldn't stop staring at this image.

I sat by the table for several minutes, drinking my home-made pain remedy, and groping the picture. Suddenly I heard the creaking of a door upstairs. Fearing Pete would catch me going through his personal belongings, I hastily gathered the papers. My sudden movement caused my head to throb with terrible pain, but I ran to the pantry, and stuffed them into the drawer. I raced back to the table just before Pete entered the kitchen.

"Oh, are you up already?" I heard the surprise in his voice.

"I have a monstrous headache, so I came down to get some painkillers."

"Did you find any? If I have some, they would be some-where in the pantry."

"I tried, but couldn't find anything."

"Then maybe I ran out of them. I've kind of used them heavily lately," said Pete, heading for the coffee maker. "I see you made some coffee."

"I had to. Someone told me that coffee with lemon works better than aspirin."

"I've never heard of that, but since you are trying it, we shall see," he said. "Or, maybe…do you want me to go and get some of the real thing from the store?"

"No, I'm getting better." I hoped he believed me, but seeing his expression, I wasn't sure about that. "We can stop at Walgreens on our way to the hospital," I added.

"Oh, Joe." Pete voice changed. "I forgot to tell you about it last night. I found a job for you. One of my friends—it's just temporary, for now at least." He paused. "We'll see how things go."

"Thanks, Pete." I said, pulling myself up from the chair. "You know how much I'll need that. Thanks again."

"Come on, Joe," said Pete. "Don't be silly. You don't have to thank me that much." His laughter held a touch of shyness. "Let's get some real breakfast. That should make us feel a little better. Then we have to see my friend Steve before noon."

Chapter 10

There were no miracles for weeks. Every time I visited Rosie in the hospital, my heart was deprived of another slice of hope. Then, at night, I wasn't able to sleep at all. My thoughts drifted into the unexplored realm of an outlandish existence, visiting long-forgotten places, or stopping at moments I didn't remember living through. It frustrated me sometimes, but mostly I was comforted—that was the only time I had with Sally and Rosie again. It was the only way to speak with them, hold them, kiss them, and be kissed. It never lasted long enough though; the mornings were the worst. When the first arrows of the sun's light penetrated the vulnerable blinds in Sally's bedroom, everything was gone, and I was left to wait the whole day until the next journey would begin. Those harsh awakenings sapped my courage to get out of bed each morning, and I tried to postpone the inevitable moment as long as possible.

Lying in bed, covered by the warm, feather comforter, I could hear Pete's muffled noises in the kitchen. I had no idea that man was so vital until I started to live with him. I had always pictured him as a person who saw life as quite uncomplicated, who didn't pay much attention to details, and accepted each day with little concern. But he proved me wrong.

Every morning, except the first, right after my return from New York, he was up first, made breakfast, and waited for me at the table with a fresh newspaper on his lap. When I finally got myself out of bed and went downstairs, I could swear he wanted to chew me out for being late. He never did such a thing, but I couldn't help feeling he wanted to. I tried to talk him out of babysitting me; I felt simply uncomfortable about that. Once or twice, I even attempted to talk about his over-protective parenting approach, but he cut the conversations off from the start.

"Don't worry, son. That's one of the things that keeps me alive," I heard him saying in a low voice.

I was not able to find a good response to a statement like that. Or maybe I didn't need one.

One day, just out of curiosity, I decided to try to beat him to the kitchen if I was able to, and started to get up very early for the next few mornings. A couple of times, I thought I had succeeded. Stillness floated inside the house, and the charcoal cloud of the night was stretched between the walls as I sneaked downstairs. But when I got to the kitchen he was already there, waiting, no matter what time it was. Finally, I gave up and just let it go.

"Hi, Pete," I said, entering the small kitchen.

"Morning." He was already pouring the coffee. He nodded at the skillet on the range. "Eggs are getting cold; sit down."

Obeying his command, I sat and waited until he placed the pan in the middle of the table, and started filling my plate. I knew Pete wouldn't be satisfied dumping only one or two scoops of thick, loaded scrambled eggs in front of me.

"Anything new in the world?" I said between bites.

"It depends what you mean by the world," he said with a smile. "In the big world out there," he waved his hand to make sure I got the picture that he was talking about something outside these walls, "it's all the same old stuff—politics, money, and greed. That's all that counts nowadays." He paused. "Oh, maybe just a little bit of entertainment and sports—" He sipped his coffee. "But it's still money, greed, and politics." He laughed. "These things never change."

"And I assume they never will—" I said but he didn't let me finish.

"But if you are asking about our world, I don't have an answer. They didn't write about that in here." He pointed at the newspaper he pushed to the side.

"I know," I said. "Sometimes I think they should. Maybe that would help."

"Nothing is going to help unless you are ready to accept the facts. No magical healing pill will take care of all your problems. But let me say this, there is something that gives us the courage to stand up against everything, no matter how bad things are—"

"Well," I said. "I know exactly what you want to say. I have heard it so many times before—faith, isn't it?"

"If you have it, you don't need anything else."

"That's easy for you to say," I said, "but what can I have a faith in?" I didn't wait for an answer. "Besides the fact that my wife is dead, and my daughter is a...vegetable. Everything else is really fine...almost perfect." I paused longing for air. "My life is so screwed up," I said, trying not to use the more graphic word I thought would be more appropriate. "I have nothing to live for."

Pete moved the newspaper. He leaned over the table. Our eyes met for the first time in weeks.

"Remember that Sally was my daughter," he whispered. "And Rosie is as important to me as she is to you. I am in pain as much as you are, if not more. Do you know what is it to lose your only child? Do you?" He looked at me again. "But I am not giving up; I won't—"

"Pete, I didn't mean to—"

"Don't apologize. That's not going to change anything. Just make sure you get your head straight. You have plenty to live for." I could feel his fierce gaze drilling me. "Rosie is alive. And as long as God wants, she will stay alive. Who are we to question His decisions?" Pete stepped back. "Everything is up to Him. Everything."

I watched Pete with an awe. It took me quite a while to get up the courage to ask, "Where do you get this kind of confidence? Were you always this way?"

"No," he said with a smile, suddenly calm again, "I wasn't, but I have learned." He sat back down. "I have had my share of doubt, but I have learned."

I waited but he didn't say anything else. We sat across from each other and shared a long moment of silence. Here sat a man who lost the love of his life when Sally was just seven years old.

Now he was a father whose only daughter had tragically passed away, and the grandfather of a child who was left in a coma after an accident with unknown chances of survival. I couldn't believe he was giving me a lecture about faith. Faith? In whom? God? Didn't he feel abandoned by God, who, in all His wisdom, had taken everything most precious away from him? Hadn't God served him a bitter life in which the few moments of happiness he had, were mere excuses to inflict more pain and suffering? How bold was it to test him so much and at the same time require total subordination, and devotion beyond reasonable doubt?

I wasn't ready to comprehend it. It was so mysterious to me, so thorny, that I nearly spoke out and questioned Pete's irrational beliefs. But I didn't. I didn't feel strong enough to start an argument with a man who was so blinded by his beliefs that he didn't see it was one big joke of the Almighty Creator. That the greatest and most powerful Being in the universe played with our lives in ways He found amusing, and simultaneously, still demanded inclusive loyalty. Slowly, without saying a word, I stood up, and walked to the door. I waited a few seconds, expecting a Pete's reaction, before I pulled the handle. The whine of the hinges cut the colorless air, then flew away into the cold.

I was already late for work but I didn't care. It had nothing to do with a lack of gratitude for the opportunity to earn money. Steve was the owner of a small construction company and maintenance service. I was grateful for all the projects he had "accidentally" run across lately and for the income it provided me. I was indebted to Steve and his wife, Harriet—though I suspected it might be her idea to keep me employed. I wasn't the greatest worker; as a matter of fact, I have never been a very good carpenter. I would grade myself as average, if I had to. But right then, I was fully conscious of the fact that I was probably closer to being the worst worker they had ever hired.

During those few weeks since I moved to Fox River Valley Gardens, and began to "work" for Steve, I couldn't stop myself from thinking about the variety of tasks they found for me. I assumed they were assigned to me out of sympathy, and not because they actually needed to be done. Of course, no one said anything, but I sensed it. Everyone I met was so nice and supportive that I was very close to getting fed up with all of that kindness. Why can't they just act normal? I didn't want their pity; I didn't want their support—maybe that much wasn't true. But if only I could liberate myself, and not be dependent on them, I would. My rudeness probably would wound their hearts if they could see through me, and I was sorry for my faults, but I was just trying to survive and go on. I wanted to forget everything that had happened.

Apparently, it wasn't meant to be. I was not able to stop thinking about it. More and more often, that strange feeling of closeness between us became perceptible. When the hiss of the sleek nail gun I used pierced two-by-fours with the galvanized nails as easily as stabbing a watermelon flesh, my mind wandered. The clean solution grew on me every time I heard the nail gun's soothing sound. One simple whisper of condensed air, a little sting in the temple, and then…everything would be so easy. So calm, so quiet, so easy…

"Hey, Joe!" I heard Steve's voice. He ran toward my truck. "Thank God. We were starting to worry."

Not again, please, I thought as I rolled up my window. "I'm sorry. Pete made me stay longer," I said loudly. "Sorry."

"Don't worry. How is—"

"She's the same." I was already out of the car, the door slamming behind me. "Let's go, shall we?"

We entered another of the monstrous cookie-cutter houses being built in one of the Valley's sprawling subdivisions. It seemed to me like someone had deliberately set out to destroy the natural beauty of the countryside with modern pseudo-castle homes for wannabes. I didn't care for the ridiculous modern necessities, and sometimes tried to search the reasoning behind the cover-page façade. But who was I to judge the infallible plans and decisions of county authorities? I had heard that at least half of the developments in the area belonged to family members, or the close friends of a certain high-ranking official. I didn't make anything out of that, but I took note of the rumor.

Inside the naked shell, the chilly breeze played hide-and-seek around the wooden skeleton of the house. The roofers had already begun their circus-like dance with plywood sheets above us. I could hear the whisper of kerosene heaters in other parts of the site where the rest of the crew tried to assemble a provisional workbench in the middle of the unfinished living room, and prepared pieces of wood to be cut. The guys glanced up as we approached, and shot puzzled looks at Steve, then they saw me. Immediately, their eyes dropped, hiding their fear, as if they could get burned or cursed just by a sight of me. Except for the casual, stifled, "Hi, Joe," they didn't say more.

Great start of yet another fabulous day, I thought, and I tried to lighten the atmosphere by saying, "What's up, guys? Who gets the pain-in-the-ass helper today?"

They all laughed, but I was fully aware I was barely scratching the surface of an invisible barricade that grew around me, and bounded me inside. Most of the people I'd met recently—whether we knew each other or were perfect strangers—were terrified by my presence. I couldn't see the reason why it was happening, or maybe I didn't care to understand. Considering my own behavior, I probably would act the same way they did. The pain-in-the-ass part was certainly true in every way.

Frank was the self-appointed supervisor, a man who thought that he possessed all knowledge of every aspect of construction field; he played along with my self-evaluation.

"You're going to work with me, Joe-boy. Let's give those guys a break, OK?"

I looked at Steve.

"That's up to you," said Steve. "I still have some paperwork to do. I'll see you all later."

Everybody stood quiet, nearly motionless, each man holding tight his breath. I was sure they were honestly afraid that Frank could change his decision and ask one of them to partner with the leper. I tried to read their thoughts by their expressions, but I couldn't. Their eyes searched the room, careful to avoid even the slightest proximity to me.

"You're the boss," said Brian, breaking the silence. He was the oldest man in the pack, and he always managed to stand behind the others. "But let me borrow him for today, Frank. I could sure use some help with that fireplace framing on the second floor."

This was a little strange to me. I had never exchanged even a word with Brian. I didn't think it was me; it just happened that way. I had a feeling that he, like almost everyone, had been avoiding me too. So why now?

Frank thought about Brian's request for a moment. "OK," he finally said. "Joe, go with Brian, and the rest of you get the hell back to work." He took a few steps then turned back. "Don't even think about another break before noon, Jeff. You get it?"

A short, heavy, tired middle-aged man in a dirty coverall murmured something inaudible.

Except for exchanging some measurements or cutting in-structions, we mutely worked together until the lunch break. It was much better than I anticipated—peace and quiet. But as we were just about to break for lunch, and go down to join the others, Brian grabbed my arm and turned me around to face him. It wasn't a very gentle move, rather a violent yank. I didn't know what to expect. I didn't know what he wanted from me, but I held my ground tautly, and prepared my defense. A jolt of uneasiness charged through my body, and fear squeezed the rest of the air from my lungs.

"Listen, Joe, I know we don't know each other," said Brian, each word rough and broken. "And I know that you might not care for what I want to say to you."

"I don't want—" I started but he didn't let me finish.

"But I want you to hear this, regardless of what you'll think of me." All the time he was grasping my arm, cutting off my blood circulation. "I know what you are afraid of the most..." Unlike most people, his eyes didn't run from contact with me.

"Oh, really? You do?" I said. What the hell does he want? What is this about? I added in my thoughts.

"Yes, and if you give me a second—"

"Go ahead." I didn't want to but decided to play along. I'd been through so much already, what more could possibly happen? I steadied myself to take whatever was coming. "Shoot."

Brian let go of my arm and backed up a little. I rubbed my bicep—I could still feel his clenched fingers. It seemed he was capable of chopping down a tree with his bare hands.

"You're not afraid of what happened," he said. "You are not afraid of the past—it's gone. As for the present, you are in pain; you know that already. And the future, we both know we have no control over it. What you are really afraid of is what you might discover." He paused. "That's all I wanted to say...," he added softly.

He circled around me and started walking down the temporary stairs. I didn't know what to say. I didn't expect to hear anything like that from him. From my father-in-law, yes—it would be more predictable. But Brian? I met him not too long ago, and had never spoken with him before.

Why him? What was that about? Who the hell does he think he is? I thought I was a good judge of character. Evidently I wasn't. I was worried to even reflect on how many others I had underestimated in the past. Too many to count, I was sure about that.

I took off earlier than usual. Of course, Frank hadn't minded my late arrival, and naturally he also let me go without question. I used the visit to the hospital as an excuse, and it was not entirely a lie. I was planning to see Rosie anyway this evening. But first I had to do something else. Everything came together after lunch—during long hushed moments broken only by short comments passed between Brian and me. It unexpectedly hit me while playing with the beloved nail gun. I didn't recognize it right away; the thought simmered while I shot a few rounds of the nails ferociously through the wood. But then I understood. It was the only thing that could possibly help me right now. I didn't know why I hadn't done it before, but that was irrelevant at the moment. My only thought was to get there as soon as possible.

I walked through the field of souls not long before dusk covered its hollow dwellings. A small sign at the entrance told me that the cemetery gate would close in half an hour. It didn't matter.

I hadn't been here since Sally's funeral. My courage wasn't running high throughout this period, neither was my memory, so I had some problems locating her grave. In addition, many new permanent tenants had checked in, further confusing the issue. I had never considered how fast we could turn into a pile of insignificant dust. Since I had let Pete take care of everything, I nearly forgot that he had mentioned something about planning to put an obelisk, or a marker, on her site. I just accepted it without a question; I knew I wasn't very helpful, but it was just too much for me.

I indistinctly recalled Pete's words that it would be similar, so I started to search for something like the headstones I had seen on the graves of Sally's mother and grandmother. When I was pretty sure I was near the right plot, I found a narrow alley with walls of granite monuments in all directions. There were no lamps at the cemetery so, guided only by the fading sun, I moved slowly around the graves. After yet another passage through the valley of stones, I noticed one empty parcel between two of the biggest family vaults I had ever seen. I didn't remember them, and I wondered how I could have missed such unique constructions. On the other hand, I was being too hard on myself—I had missed more than that. Everything about that evening was blurred.

I approached the open space with caution, convinced I'd found her. As I came within a few feet, it became obvious I was right. My only light scarcely hung in the sky, and lit the white rough-rounded marble boulder, causing the subtle dark disturbances that ran in horizontal lines to appear even darker, almost black. It looked identical to those headstones I saw so long ago, yet somehow it was different. Notwithstanding the lack of Sally's picture attached, it was something else. I couldn't make out what it was. Perhaps the night was playing cruel tricks on my perception. I stared at the bare rock, and felt the crisp surface beneath my fingertips. The letters were small and straight, but deeply engraved.

"Sally Clatt 02/16/1959 — 01/24/2000 God bless you."

Although scratched by the cold, rough edges, my palms were not ready to let it go, not yet. Leaning over the precious stone, I spent a few minutes with Sally. I could spend much more time, even my entire life here—I wouldn't care if my heart stopped at that very moment. I thought I would be much happier; everything would be uncomplicated, defined, and less demanding.

But it didn't stop. The low groan of the wooden gate being pushed closed echoed through the cemetery, signaling the end to another day. I was trying to let go of Sally, but I couldn't. I was chained to her grave, invisible shackles biting into the flesh on my wrists. But it didn't hurt. I wore the restraints willingly, one irrational part of me wanting to stay here and embrace the surprising warmth of its coarse layer.

"I trust you, Sally. As always," I said. "I'll do it. You'll see. I'll do it."

Chapter 11

The gory rays of a dying late spring sun were long gone, deflected by the billowy carpet of clouds. However, I could feel the sting of sunlight piercing the fuselage right above my head. I was under the impression that no one else was witnessing that never-ending episode of defeat of the star, except maybe an ash-haired woman, sitting three rows ahead, whose face shone with excitement. The others simply didn't care. Aware of the outcome, they were not interested in the progress of the battle. In the dimmed light covering the board, their eyes shone, sunk into sleek screens mounted in the back of the chairs in front of them. Connected to their spheres via the earphones, their lips trembling with the cheer for the artificial heroes, they have lived the oblivious dream of the in-progress algorithmic era. If not for the loud snores overlapping from time to time from the monotonous growl of the engines, I could swear I was surrounded by cyborgs.

I couldn't sleep at all; nothing gave me respite, even temporarily. I turned away from the window and watched my neighbors for a while. A couple of overgrown tourists in their fifties started the trip with the rustle of ripped cellophane as they opened the first bag of chips. Maps and guidebooks overflowed their squat backpacks tucked between their feet. They wore matching Hawaiian shirts and red baseball caps with the logo of a team I was not familiar with.

After opening their fifth bag of chips, I stopped counting. If that's all it took to make them happy, who was I to offer them nutritional advice? They probably already had more than their share of helpful suggestions. I tried hard to ignore the crunching of potato chips and looked outside the oval window, as the dark side of the earth accepted us into its arms.

It was late into the second leg of the flight when I finally achieved some semblance of stability without worrying about such things as falling from thirty thousand feet in a metal casket. It wasn't about death itself. I was more than prepared. I had only one problem—with its term, if anything. Only nineteen hours ago, I was tucked into my only just established comfort zone, or at least I thought I was. Suddenly, I found myself on an airplane. Then, I wandered in the strange labyrinth that was the overbuilt Amsterdam airport, and one connecting flight later, I still lacked purpose.

The whole thing just found me unguarded. A fast discussion with Pete and the next thing I knew, I was on board—quick, painless, and sweet. The bitterness came later. I couldn't complain too much about Pete not being able to find a nonstop flight; he held the budget in his hands. I was merely the recipient, and even though I wanted to chip in the money I had saved, he didn't allow it.

"You'll have better ways to spend it after you get back," he said. "You can't refuse. It's a gift." He smiled. "Besides, everything is already settled," he added.

"But it's too much, Pete. I can't accept it."

"Yes, you can," he said, holding out a travel envelope containing the plane ticket. "And you should. You need to."

"But—" Pete stopped me before I could say anything else, and pushed the ticket into my hands. It almost fell to the floor, but I caught it in midair.

"Look it over. We can't change the departure date, unfortunately…" He took a step in my direction. "But the return date is flexible, I set it for this Saturday, but you can change it anytime. Just call the airline."

"I won't," I said. "It won't be necessary. Five days should be enough for…" I wasn't sure what I would be looking for out there. Sally's letter didn't specify any reason, and Pete wasn't helpful on that issue. It was one thing to accept Sally's last wish, but quite another to figure out what it meant.

"What am I going to do once I get there, Pete?" It wasn't the first time when I raised the question. "Tell me. If you can just give me a hint, I'd appreciate it, because this doesn't make any sense to me."

"What doesn't?" asked Pete.

"France, Sally's request, everything," I said. "She never had anything to do with France as far as I remember!"

"Why would you say that?" said Pete, observing me carefully.

"She never mentioned anything—" I paused. "Well…maybe once or twice about her distant family connections. But it was vague, and it seemed so unimportant."

"Well," said Pete, "maybe it wasn't as unimportant as you think. Maybe you didn't listen well. Nothing ring a bell?"

"What are you trying to say?"

He didn't answer, and after a long pause he said while taking a little step back. "Did you trust her?" He was studying me.

"What?"

"Did you trust your wife, I asked?"

"Of course I did." Once I said that, I was certain where Pete was going.

"So, why don't you trust her one more time?" he said.

"I want to, but—"

"There is no 'but,' Joe," said Pete, grabbing my hand. "Look at me." He stepped forward. He was a little bit taller than me, and standing close, inches from each other, his appearance wasn't as good as I thought. Once handsome, reflecting his personality, his face was now marred with deep valleys of tired wrinkles...

"Believe in Sally, and she will guide you," he said, as he let go of me, and swiftly changed the subject. "Oh, I made car and hotel reservations for you."

What the hell was he talking about? What was supposed to ring a bell? What does this have to do with the trip? I thought, but I didn't say a word, just stood silently, hesitant, and willing to accept everything that was being offered.

"Oh...about the hotel." Pete smiled. "It would be rather hard to call it a hotel, although they love to use that name."

"Pete how—" I said, but he ignored me.

"It's more of a bed and breakfast, small but clean, right in the center of the village. It should be nice; a friend recommended it, and I have been—"

"A friend?" Somehow I was dubious. "Pete, have you ever been—" He didn't let me finish.

"Everything is in there, the address of the hotel," he said as he flashed a square yellow notepad card. I noticed it contained the phone number too. "Your ticket, car rental reservation, even a map—I tried to trace the best route for you." He pointed at the manila envelope. "Remember to keep it with you all the time."

Everything that had happened to me during the last few months—the drunk in the woods, money wonders in Greenpoint, the weird conversation with Brian at work, and Pete—was enough. It might be truth, I was a dummy, and I couldn't connect the dots, and nothing rang the bell, but I have decided. No more questions, he wouldn't help me answer them anyway, nobody would.

Whatever happens, no one will be able to explain. Remember, Joe, you can understand only if you really want to. But you have to do it on your own. It passed in front of my eyes. I had to take everything in my hands. I shuffled the papers, extracted the plane ticket, and slid it inside my passport. Then I closed the envelope, and placed it neatly on top of my clothes in the small suitcase—one of those bags that resembled a flight attendant's rolling travel case, and zipped it up. I won't need these until I get there.

* * *

I stood in the vibrant vestibule of the strange airport, trying to gather my thoughts. My first impression of the Marseilles air terminal was that it was poorly ventilated. My senses were accosted by humid sea air mixed with the odor of thousands of moving bodies. I hopped on the escalator leading down to baggage claims. Why have I even come to France? What am I supposed to do? What should I be looking for?

I was honoring Sally's last request. It was very important to me to fulfill it, and that was the only reason I came here. But I couldn't stop thinking about its meaning. As important as it was, it didn't make any sense to me.

Why? And what? Those two questions tortured my jet-lagged brain. I had nothing to rely on, except one piece of information Pete gave me before I left. Supposedly, but I didn't think it was entirely the truth, not a complete lie, but not a total truth, either, his friend provided him the address of my destination—the cute bed and breakfast somewhere down south in Cote d'Azur, one of the small villages. That was all, I had nothing else to go on. No route of retreat, no backup plans. Everything was as crazy as jumping into a well and counting on someone's word that the water was there, and even crazier—forgetting to verify if the chain with the bucket was attached, just in case.

I walked through the spacious terminal, searching for signs to the luggage carousel. At least they used some English. If not for that, I would probably be here forever. I didn't pack many things, just necessities. My only luggage, the black suitcase, was small enough to fit in the overhead compartment of the plane. I was sure. I compared it to the display back in Chicago.

But a growling attendant took it away from me while I was trying to board the plane. One of those overly friendly flight attendants put a stop on it and directed one of the vultures with the airport security clearance badges to take it down to the luggage deck. My protests were hopeless; she even didn't pay any attention to me, just grabbed it in exchange for a crumpled cardboard voucher. I shrugged. I had my plane ticket with the boarding pass, passport, and my wallet with me so I could live without the suitcase. The only thing I forgot to take out was the manila envelope with all the information Pete gave me. I felt a little wave of panic when I imagined the remote possibility of my suitcase landing in a different part of the globe by accident.

I kept my fingers crossed as I approached a group of passengers, and spotted the chip lovers from the plane. I double-checked the flight number and the city of departure—Amsterdam—displayed above the squeaky carousel. I leaned over the luggage carts nearby, and examined bags as they snaked by on the conveyor. After more than an hour of waiting, when only the memories of the suitcases, backpacks, and bags played on the rubber boards of the carousel, I accepted the fact that my suitcase must be missing. I gave up.

I was lucky to spot the "Luggage Service" sign nearby, and rushed in the direction the sharp arrow was pointing. They must need that often, I bet. It took only a few more signs and turns to get around the last corner. In the blind end of the terminal, I found a small booth with the suitcase logo on the window. Next to the transparent booth, there were rows of chairs, all of them awaiting fresh occupants, laid in order inside an enclosure of three tall frosted glass-block walls. I was so absorbed in the quest to find my suitcase that I didn't pay attention to what was happening. The glass door of the booth soundlessly opened when I pushed it, and I stepped inside. It seemed that no one was there, but I approached the desk anyway.

Just as my hands hit the countertop, like a jack-in-the-box, a young man neatly uniformed in indigo, popped out from behind the counter.

"Bonsoir, que puis-je faire pour vous?"

"Je ne parle pas français," I said, consulting a cheat sheet from my pocket. "English," I poked my chest with my fingers. "English."

"Oh, oui, oui." He smiled. "How may I help you?" His voice sung with the traditional English accent.

"I think I lost my suitcase, I mean, you lost my suitcase." I scratched my head. "I'm sorry, it's not your fault. It got lost—"

"Do not worry please, Monsieur. I am here to assist you. May I see your ticket, please?"

I placed the travel envelope with the ticket and the boarding pass on the counter. He assessed the attached sticker, and in seconds, I heard the clatter of a keyboard, hidden somewhere below the top of the counter. I lost track of time as he waged a ferocious battle with the buttons, and I patiently waited for the outcome.

"Excusez-moi, Monsieur Clatt."

"Yes? What happened?"

"According to my information, everything is fine. There was a little mistake in the system, but your suitcase is here, and I will go and retrieve it for you. I shall be back in a few minutes."

"Thank you," I said.

"Not a problem, Monsieur Clatt. You shall sit down and relax, please." He pointed to the rows of chairs outside his little chamber. "It should not take long."

We walked out and I headed for the first chair right in front of his booth.

"Bienvenue en France—welcome in France, Monsieur Clatt." He added and departed into the emptiness of the terminal.

I faced the enclosure with rows of plastic chairs of an indeterminate shade. I had expected some vivid color in this European port, but all I saw was neutral. I looked up. For a moment, I was sincerely afraid I had become color blind. I wasn't able to distinguish any color in the building; everything seemed to be painted flat. After a while, I accepted the fact that different shades of gray performed in front of me, and I blamed the long trip for my condition, hoping it would be only temporary. It was surprising that I didn't spot anyone in the immediate area. I found it amusing to be the only unlucky chump tonight. I heard muffled echoes of a commotion in the farthest part of the terminal, but no one was approaching this lost corner.

I didn't think twice about what to do. I sat down with a thump. I was worn out, and all I had dreamed about for the last few hours was a hot shower and a bed, any bed. Any level, flat area big enough to fit me would do. The chilly iron floor started to appear very inviting, and I could hardly refrain from sliding down from the hollow of the plastic chair to stretch out on it.

I assumed Pete was waiting for my call, but my legs were not responding to the phone search issued by my brain. I examined the leaden wall clock—midnight was approaching painfully slowly. In that part of my memory, which was still somehow functioning, I tried to calculate the time difference between Marseilles and Chicago, and I confirmed it with my watch. I didn't move after happily realizing that with the seven-hour difference, it was only before five in the afternoon back home. I decided to call Pete later, right after the resolution of my suitcase matter. I was sure I must have passed one of those telephone kiosks on my way here. I straightened my legs and my eyelids slammed closed like broken garage doors.

I felt a soft touch on my hand, the gentle touch of smooth warm skin that immediately reminded me of Sally. I jumped, but when I opened my eyes, the only thing I saw was a smiling attendant, his mouth twisted in a troubled curve.

"I am very sorry, Monsieur Clatt," he whispered. "I tried very hard but unfortunately, I was not able to find your suitcase. There must be some kind of mistake in the system. It appears that your luggage was mishandled and has not arrived here yet. I am very sorry."

"What?" His words caught me off guard.

"No luggage, Monsieur Clatt. I could not locate it." His smile, his entire expression, was so professional I had a hard time comprehending what this meant. "I will have to do more research. Contact Northwest Airlines—"

"So do it," I shouted, and then added, "please."

"Yes, of course Monsieur Clatt, I shall make it priority first thing in the morning," said the attendant.

"Morning?"

"Tomorrow, Monsieur Clatt." The proficient smile shone on his face. "It's—"

"What do you mean by tomorrow? What's wrong with today?" I heard a throbbing sound right behind my ears.

"I am very sorry, Monsieur Clatt." His face didn't correspond with the sympathetic tone of his voice. "My shift has just has come to an end. I shall go home."

"Well, I get it, but how about your replacement?" I said, trying to maintain a glimmer of hope.

"Who, Monsieur Clatt?"

"The person who comes to work the next shift when you go home." I couldn't say it clearer.

"Oh, oui," he said. "No one comes."

"What do you mean? No one is coming? So what is going to happen? What about other people who arrive here tonight?"

"There is a little chance of that. There shouldn't be any more flights until early the morning. In any case, the airport is accessible twenty-four hours, and if there will be someone requiring our services, they will have to return in the morning when we open. We close at midnight."

"So, what about me?" I tried to play the begging note. "Are you going to leave me without any help?"

"I am really sorry, Monsieur Clatt. We are closed," he said, pointing to the little sign that hung on the glass wall next to the door. "We are open from six in the morning to midnight. That is eighteen hours." His whole body was searching for my compassion and acceptance. "In addition, the airline counters have already closed. Please understand that there is nothing I could do anyway. Everything is closed at this time."

I was unable to relate to him, for some reason. The prospect of waiting for my suitcase until morning—if, of course, he would even be able to find it—didn't appeal to me at all.

"Come on. Do you really want me to believe that you can't find a piece of luggage after midnight?" I said.

"We are closed, Monsieur Clatt. I am sorry. Come back to-morrow morning, please. Or," he added after a pause, "we can deliver it right to your destination."

"Oh, no, no." I said quickly. "I want to make sure it will be found. I have my—"

"We shall find your suitcase for sure in the morning, I promise," he said. "Good night, Monsieur Clatt," he added, turning to beat a hasty retreat before I had a chance to say something nasty.

He left me alone in the small enclosure in this forgotten part of the airport. As it powered down, lights winking out, the Lost Luggage office became a dying patient losing its vital signs. And, all that remained was the monotonous tone of the flat line. It hung, like a broken ceiling, ready to collapse on everyone who had not run, covering them with its deadly wheeze. In spite of its threats, I was hoping someone suffering similar misfortune would come by. Then we could join forces, and beat the hidden fiend of the terminal that gobbled up luggage. But after two hours of waiting, I declared defeat.

I mulled over my options. I could try to rent a car with no reservation, and without Pete's map, and get to the hotel. But considering the time, my chances of finding the rent-a-car booth open at two in the morning were slim to none. And even if I was lucky enough to rent a car, the night drive though an unknown country without any directions whatsoever seemed a little too risky, so the alternative was effortless. I planned to stay in the terminal until morning, resolve the issue with the suitcase, retrieve all my documents, and then proceed as planned.

I was already trying to assume the most comfortable sleeping position possible on the inflexible chair when a bolt of fear ran through my mind. No, I'm not going to call Pete. I tried to fight it. Not now. What is he going to think of me? Didn't he tell me to keep the papers with me all the time?

Drained, frustrated, and frazzled by traveler's fever, I stretched out in the listless enclosure of the terminal's dreary wing and tried to avoid looking up at the frigid bearing of the fluorescent moons hanging above me. Whether I wanted to or not, I was forced to spend a beautiful night at one of Europe's largest airports with a great panoramic view of glass walls all around me; all king-size beds in the room, and so many to choose from. And I could have them all for myself. I picked the last row of six or eight plastic chairs. The bed wasn't made very well—it was as comfy as getting a deep tissue massage from an inexperienced therapist, but somehow I managed not to scream. After a while, lassitude calmed my fears, and started to work its anesthetic magic; nothing bothered me anymore. I wafted away.

Sometime later—it was hard for me to judge the hour—an odd current of cold froze my dreamless nap and carved the ethereal peace of the airport. At first, I assumed the ventilation system finally started to work, and was going awry spreading the chilled air, like in many grocery stores back home. But after a while, a feeling of uneasiness crept into my heart. Fully awake, but with my eyes still shut down, I lay half-slid down on a chair, frantically trying to figure out what had awakened me. Then I got it—it wasn't only the cold; it was a draft carrying a scent I was sure I had come into contact with before. Filled with thoughts of white pepper and salty seawater, a strong sneeze-provoking stench hit my nostrils. I sat up and searched for the cause of the odor.

The very first thing my eyes lit on was the shadowy outline of a man. Sitting in the first row of chairs on the other side of the enclosure, the little old man seemed to be sleeping too. But after a moment, I realized his eyes were wide open. I wasn't sure if he was the source of the unusual odor, but in the dimmed lights of the terminal, he was the only change I observed. What a champ! He must have gotten here after I passed out. The little old man didn't move while I evaluated the situation. His shiny eyeballs pushed a bit too far out of their sockets, but held a lifeless calm. His mouth closed, crooked in an unsatisfied smirk with just a hint of passion, and for no clear reason, promising. His long, dusty hair stuck together at the ends, nonetheless managed to look impressive. His light brown trench coat flowed over his chair with a waterfall of sandy, irregular stripes. His shirt blended in perfectly, although it obviously used to sparkle. I couldn't see his pants, but judging from the mileage on the shoes sticking out at the hem of the trench coat, I could imagine.

Was he homeless, someone who just happened to be in the area and tried to steal some luxury for one night? A beggar who lost track of time, and wasn't aware the last possible customers were gone for the day? I didn't know. Considering his appearance, that certainly could be the case. But I sensed something else. I couldn't find an explanation for my feeling—some indefinable quality did not correspond with the man I saw in front of me. The little old man possessed dignity. I could feel the strength that made him seem noble. Even in those tired clothes, he had something royal in him. I wasn't sure what that was.

I decided to say something, though I wasn't confident he would understand English, when I realized that there was someone else sitting behind him. What? I'm sure he was there alone a second ago. But apparently I was mistaken.

Dark contours of at least two people were clearly visible. I shook my head in disbelief; as if asking a wordless question, I pointed my hand at the old man. But still—perfect serenity. Once again, looking at the man, I noticed that whoever was there just seconds ago was gone— there was no one in the row behind him. I swiveled my head around, searching for them, but they were nowhere to be seen. I glanced at the little old man again, and started to doubt myself. Two people were sitting next to the man, one on each side of him, silent and staring. I couldn't see them clearly; the view was blurred, like someone stretched a filter, a thin silk screen, between us. But I was able to see the little old man's face in detail. I moved my eyes to his companions and again, my vision smudged. I couldn't even fathom a guess as to who they were. They were nothing but formless human contours.

Tranquility played a deafening tone in my ears, and the peppery smell blocked by the glass walls filled the whole enclosure. In the last call for my sanity, I decided to face those people, and stood up, but before I made a step forward, I had to sit down. I got a glimpse of yet another person now sitting in the row right behind the group. It disturbed me only for a moment. I made sure the old man was still sitting in his seat—he hadn't moved. The rest were there too, and they watched me. I couldn't help it—I simply panicked. I tried to cry for help, but my voice failed me, as if it was erased from a live soundtrack. I remained mute and unable to move. The temperature of my body must've melted the plastic chair and fuse me with it. The part of my brain that wasn't occupied by the process of analyzing the situation yelled, Run! But I couldn't obey. The problem wasn't even the chair attached to my back—my feet were bonded to the floor.

I closed my eyes in the painfully slow agony of waiting for the unavoidable. I was trying not to count my respirations, but I couldn't help it—three breaths in one second. Nothing happened. I squeezed my eyelids even tighter, and waited. Nothing again. I guessed that several minutes had passed.

There wasn't a sound at all; I could hear the silence hover above me. I wasn't trying to be brave; it was beyond my control. I couldn't wait any longer, and opened my eyes. To my surprise, there was no one in the chairs. The little old man was gone, and so were his blurry friends. I was happy to see those chairs empty again. The terminal brightened with the first, shy signs of daylight.

"Don't even think about it." I said to myself. "If you want to stay sane, that is."

Chapter 12

It was a little after five in the morning when the torrent of life reanimated the airport terminal, and infused some traffic of the living around me. But it wasn't until just a few minutes before six that I finally saw someone approaching the luggage service booth. A man in his late twenties, wearing the navy blue uniform of a terminal employee, was carrying a small black suitcase. It wasn't the same young man, who tried to help me last night, but I couldn't care less—I thought I recognized my suitcase from a distance. I didn't quite see it yet, but I had that feeling in my heart. Not that I have been traveling a lot—in fact, I hadn't used any suitcase in the last decade—but I just knew it had to be mine.

And I wasn't mistaken. A few signatures later, with apologies on behalf of the airline, I left this bitter hall. After I mingled with a crowd—who I was rather sure I could touch, and they wouldn't evaporate in front of me in the noisy main terminal—I plucked up the courage to place the suitcase on a chair.

It seemed untouched, the combination lock closed tightly with no signs of tampering. I wasn't sure why someone would try to open my suitcase but there was nervous anticipation inside me when I turned the dial of the lock. I took out the manila envelope, sitting on top of my clothes and pulled out a stack of papers. The car reservation, the square yellow hand-written note from Pete with the name and address of the hotel where he had made a reservation for me, and a thick folded road map of southern France. I've should listen to Pete. Well, next time..., I promised myself. Not that I had any further travel plans; the probability of yet another trip was so remote, I laughed out loud.

I folded the rental car reservation and placed it in my back pocket. I seized the little note; its small, yellow square face stared at me blankly, as though trying to jump out of my hands. I thought I was dreaming. I turned it over and almost swore out loud. I was sure I must have taken the wrong page of the notepad, but I couldn't see how that happened.

Drops of sweat formed on my body as I berated myself for my stupidity. I'm a laughingstock! Pete will have a field day with me.

But when I calmed a little, I recalled that last evening before my departure. It was Pete who put all those papers together. I was the idiot who placed the envelope in the suitcase, but he prepared the papers. He advised me to keep the envelope with me, but, no, I had to be smarter. Would Pete accidentally give me the wrong piece of paper? I doubted that. He was too organized, too cautious to let this happen, I was more than sure. I brought the yellow square closer one more time.

This time, I examined it more thoroughly and saw that it wasn't as blank as I thought it was. I held it up to the light, using the bright ceiling lamps as a luminous background. "Saintes-Maries-de-la-Mer" was perceptible, faintly imprinted on the bottom of the note. Where is the rest? Where the hell is the address? I asked myself. I remembered seeing the name of the bed and breakfast with a street address in a strange village, and the phone number just below it. It's gone now. What happened? What am I supposed to do?

I gave the yellow note a chance again, lifting it up higher to let more light penetrate the thin paper. Now there was nothing at all on the paper. The odd name was gone too. The note was empty and seemed as untouched as a new notepad. Quickly, I flipped it over— nothing either; and the front again—still pure.

"What the——?" I said. From the corner of my eye, I saw some people glancing at me with puzzled expressions as they passed me.

After a moment, I threw the worthless note back into the envelope, grabbed the map, and shut the suitcase.

I'm going to talk to Pete about that when I call him. I checked my watch. It displayed twenty past midnight; I had forgotten to change it to the local time. Well, that can wait, I decided. With suitcase in hand, I marched toward the sign that pointed to the rental car area. At least I'll get to the village; then I'll call Pete in a few hours.

It took me much longer than I expected to get to the Saintes-Maries-de-la-Mer. Reading directions from the map was one thing, but experiencing French roads in reality was something different. The village wasn't far from Marseilles—only seventy miles or so—but I spent more than five hours in my petite burgundy rental Renault. I had never heard of that make, but obviously, it was one of the most popular cars here. There were dozens of assorted Renaults on the road. It didn't ride that badly, a little bumpy at times, but its claustrophobic size gave me a headache. And what was even worse, I felt like I was back home driving through a road construction zone. Once the highway ended, the cavalcade of cars barely moved on the curved roads that led through the marshlands toward the sea. Thousands of people must have jumped in their cars this chilly morning, and every one of them made a point of driving in the same direction. There was little traffic from the opposite way. A few sped by, with—I was sure—laughing drivers.

Without even a seed of a plan, I got stuck behind a spring-green Volkswagen minivan from the sixties or seventies. It was loaded with people dressed in eccentric, vibrant-hued clothing, and filled with a haze of teal smoke. I was trying to stay awake, and didn't have the energy to contemplate my fellow travelers. I tried the radio, but it didn't do any good.

Accidentally, I found a few stations broadcasting in English; I didn't care much for their music. Unfortunately, I had trouble understanding the DJs on the rest of the dial, but at least turning the knob back and forth every few minutes occupied me enough to keep me alert. After a while, the channel surfing struck me as funny.

At last, I drove into the small village, which certainly was the final destination of the endless caravan of cars. I crawled through the center of the village with a speed of a racing snail. Through the cramped, rugged streets, the blend of people and cars rushed in every possible direction like a lively rainbow. I quickly found that there wasn't a parking space to be had. Whatever will be—will be. I promised myself to take it one step at a time.

The village was packed. Human and machine were scrambled together in an incomprehensible symbiosis. All the village's streets were full; cars were parked everywhere, including the sidewalks, and people dodged to escape them. The only crowd-free space I could discern was the azure of the Mediterranean Sea, visible in the distance.

I was stuck inside the car, slowly starting to boil, though this was more from anticipation than the sun. I found a big A/C switch bullying its way clear on the dashboard of the foolish little car, but rolled down the window instead. The cool and breezy air helped, but even then, I couldn't figure out my next step. I had to get out, but it was impossible to tell when and where that would be in this crush. I couldn't last much longer, and hoped that a parking space would materialize where I could dump this motorized confinement. The matured, green VW van was stubbornly stuck in front of me, heaving ahead as its driver ignored the jam-packed roadway.

After a long few minutes, I was ready to abandon my vessel somewhere between the boutique store with a big display window and a small coffee shop with a few chairs spread on the scanty walkway. But I changed my mind. I decided to follow the van. I don't know where I'm going anyway, so what's the difference? At least it seemed like a start.

The antique Volkswagen swayed through the village right toward the sea as if the driver knew precisely what he was doing. For a moment, I thought we were going to end up on the beach, but the road turned sharply and led us along the sapphire water.

After a short, yet time-consuming drive, we came to a stop before entering a large grassy camping area. Like the village, it was filled to the maximum with anything that could be used to travel. Small and large vans, campers, cars, even horses, were parked between the tents and trailers, spotting the grass without a pattern. Old-fashioned caravans proudly stood in the center of the temporary settlement. They were made out of plain wood planks painted in a variety of colors, from bright lemon to apple red to autumn brown and had uncomfortable large wooden wheels resting on the grass after a long journey. Heavy shutters hung on each side of the tiny windows, most of them open and filled with curious faces. Those who couldn't fit into one of the windows climbed the wooden steps leading to the door located on one of the shorter sides.

A brawny black-haired man approached the van and leaned in through the open window. The curled forest of hair on his torso was visible beneath a cream unbuttoned shirt. After a moment, he let the van through. I was right behind it, fully prepared to be turned away. Perhaps guarding the only parking space left in the village, the man waved me through right after the colorful Volkswagen. Lucky me, I laughed. He must have thought we were together. I was trying to keep up with the minivan, but lost it in the muddle. I had to be particularly vigilant because of the herds of children scampering around my vehicle.

After a few minutes of navigating inside the unorthodox camping ground, I found enough free space to park; not that my Renault needed much. I got out of the car and found myself in the midst of a crowd of unfamiliar people, drifting aimlessly. A puff of air, dashing from the windswept sea, swiftly washed away all signs of fatigue in one swipe.

I left my car somewhere in the middle of the lake of vehicles, with little hope that I would be able to find it later. Following the energetic crowd, I took a path along the sea leading back to the village. It was an exceptional feeling, walking next to shiny cobalt water, so innocent, so calm on the surface. I saw its bubbly white-caps, apathetically grab the polished crystals of sand and carry them away to the depths, only to throw them back moments later.

As I was approaching one of the stone arches leading to the center of the village, there was a commotion on the opposite side of the street. A few people, balancing on wooden ladders, tried to assemble some kind of flower decoration over the wall, and others, standing down below safely on the paved walkway, yelled out directions. Those on the ladders were not quiet either. Every time someone shouted from the ground, they shrieked back. Spectators cheered them on, but it was hard to say which group had more supporters.

Even though the passage was packed, its cool shadows were refreshing. I had to think twice about leaving it's antique embrace. I caught nothing more than a glimpse of a crumpled miniature of a man before I was caught up and carried away by the steady current of bodies. Not taller than five feet, razor thin, and concealed in a fawn suit, he was like a chameleon against the wall. He reminded me of a bas-relief, if not for his eyes. The only truly remarkable thing about him was his eyes. They couldn't be camouflaged. Surrounded by mocha irises, his razor pupils infiltrated anyone passing by. Those eyes never lingered too long on a subject, capturing an image and moving on. When they located me, the mental picture was taken, developed, and stored. I kept going, watching as the crowd swallowed the tiny man.

After a few hours of crossing the medieval streets, I thought I had visited all the hotels, motels, bed-and-breakfasts, and mom-and-pop boarding houses in the village. All I heard from any proprietor who spoke English was "no room." In most cases, when no one understood what I was asking, sign language worked like a charm. But it didn't help at all—every time the result was the same, a hopeless wave of empty hands accompanied by a polite smile.

Exhausted, I gave up. Walking back toward a parking lot on the outskirts of the village, I finally decided to call Pete. I was dispirited by the thought of spending another night roughing it. I wasn't sure of anything, not even the location of the nearest phone.

I felt a sharp tug from behind, as if someone was trying to tear off the sleeve of my shirt. Spinning around, I swung instinctively, but my fist only cut the air. I gasped in surprise, unable to see my attacker, and lost my balance. Only someone's heavy grasp saved me from falling on the ground. I looked down and saw him. The little man from the arch seemed to be even shorter than when I first saw him. The chameleon man, in the same yellowish suit, pulled my sleeve again with ferocity, like he wasn't just trying to get my attention—he seriously wanted a piece of my shirt.

"What is it with you?" I said, prying his gaunt fingers off my arm. "If you're asking for money, you're out of luck. I—"

"I do not ask for money." The deep tone of his voice was a comic contradiction to his posture. It seemed like it didn't belong to him; someone else must have dubbed it, perfectly synchronizing it with the movement of his lips.

"Américain?" he added, pointing his finger at me.

"Yes, American," I answered automatically.

"Merde," he said with deep relief.

"What did you say?" I asked, but he didn't answer. "What do you want from me?" I stepped back, but he moved in sync with me.

"The room? That is what you look for?" he asked, shaking his finger.

"How did you know?" I asked, feeling a little wave of stupidity. I could answer the question myself.

"Everybody need a room today," he said with a shrug.

"I know," I said, without hiding my growing frustration. "I need one too, but I have a reservation. I just lost the information, and I have to call—"

"How do you lost?" He cut me off.

"What?"

"Information. How do you lost?"

I gave him my most "it's-none-of-your-business" glare. I was not accustomed to sharing the details of my private life with perfect strangers. But there was something intriguing about this man. Some unseen quality in the man led me to rely on him. I gave in to his rough chameleon charm.

"It disappeared," I drawled syllables. "At least that's what I think. I must've spilled something on the paper."

For a second I thought I saw the glimmer of a smile, but when I fixed my eyes on him closely, his stony face was noncommittal.

"Why are you asking me all of this?" I said after a short pause.

"Not to worry. No harm," he answered, and this time, he did smile. "My name is Jean–Paul Laroche." He extended his hand, dry and coarse like a branch of an old tree. I shook it automatically. "A clean and cozy room is waiting for you at my hotel," he added.

"What are you talking about? I asked everywhere. All I know is that my hotel was supposed to be located in the center of the village, and I think I visited them all."

"You missed one, Monsieur," he said with calmness in his tenor voice. "That's why I am here."

"No, wait, wait." I was taken aback. "Do you mean to tell me that you were looking for me on the street, and you found me in all that crowd out there, just to tell me that the room in waiting for me?" I didn't hide my disbelief. "Something is very…" I tried to find the right word, "…very suspicious here. I'm going to call my father-in-law right now and get the address."

"Not necessary to call Monsieur Roberts, Monsieur Clatt," he said as my eyes widened in speechless astonishment. "I talked to Monsieur Roberts last night when you didn't arrive. He did not think you will spend a night at the airport, but he was wrong."

"OK, I can buy that. Everything you said may be possible," I said very slowly. It was Pete who coordinated my trip, so it was believable, the chameleon man, if he really ran the hotel I had a reservation in, had his number. "But how did you find me out here? I saw you in the passage, but you didn't notice me there."

"I noticed." He frowned. "I just did not know it was you."

"So—" I didn't let go.

The little chameleon man showed me a full set of the whitest teeth I had ever seen.

"No magic," he said with the open full smile. "You see, Monsieur Clatt, we all know us here. I asked them to call when you ask for room, and they all called me. They told me who to look for then, so I came. It is simple like this."

Of course it couldn't be as simple as he was trying to make me think it was, but I didn't intend to argue with him at that time. I was too drained to dispute anything, especially with someone who was offering me a clean room. In the back of my exhausted brain, there were a few questions that bothered me. Why would he ask other hotels? How did he know I would go there? How did he know I would lose the address in the first place? But I threw my arms in the air, and said, "Fine, you win. We can go, but first I have to get my suitcase from the car. I parked—"

"Not to worry, Monsieur Clatt. I take care of that," he said as he guided me across the street. "Not to worry, Monsieur Clatt."

When we walked through the short, confined streets, we changed directions so often I was lost in minutes. All what I could feel was a fresh scent of the slumbering sea, and I heard its soothing eternal lullaby.

The Rue Portalet curved like a French roll. Jean-Paul aimed for one of the small, conjoined tenement houses. One with a faded red canopy over its glass door, and the fatigued sign with the yellowed letters "Hotel Europa" painted on it. It was a long-awaited sight, for my legs ached. I was sure I hadn't seen this hotel on my earlier search through the village. I automatically registered the house number: 16. Only then, I recalled the name of the hotel, "Europa," imprinted into the yellow notepad by Pete's weighty hand. It was there two days ago, just before I left—washed out only this morning, gone, as if it had never existed. Shut up! I reprimanded myself.

The chameleon man smiled and pointed toward the door. It didn't seem to be the bed-and-breakfast I had imagined. It was in the center of the village just as I was told, but located on a side street, which was difficult to find. The hotel was just a plain white stucco house—nothing more. It was very well camouflaged and thus, easy to miss; even the sign out front blended in. In only one detail, it resembled the mom-and-pop little house modernized to accommodate guests—it was little. The rest didn't match at all.

After a moment, I was led inside. The wing of the glass door opened with a single gentle push of Jean-Paul's hand, but smacked me severely as it closed.

"Punaise," said Jean-Paul. "You OK? I forgot they are heavy."

"I'm fine," I said, massaging my shoulder. "Don't worry about it. I'm OK. I should be more careful."

We entered the short foyer. I stopped and assessed the environment. The reception desk seemed to be as ancient and tired as the canopy outside. Mistreated by time, bleak tapestry feebly embraced the walls, and the wooden furniture was scratched and miserable. Weak carpeting led to what I took to be the dining room. A half-empty bar was visible from the entrance, and straight ahead, the hall led farther into the house. An old-fashioned clock in front of me glued the time in this place. Burned-out bulbs in many of the lamps created the dreary, dismal ambiance that almost made me bolt.

But at the same time, I perceived all that bleakness around me from a quite different angle. Concealed under the surface of disrepair, I was able to see a grand, dignified guesthouse where only well-chosen guests were privileged to stay. I didn't have time to follow that line of thought. My petite French host went behind the small reception desk and grabbed a key from one of the pigeonholes on the shelf attached to the back wall.

"Let's go up, Monsieur Clatt," he said, pointing the key toward the worn stairs that sprouted next to the reception desk.

I let him lead the way, and slowly took the first step up the dim staircase. With each tread, my drained body bawled for help—a few hours of sleep in the horizontal position was so close; only that thought kept me from collapsing. My host opened the last door in the long but compressed hallway and turned on the single light, inviting me in.

"Here you go, Monsieur Clatt," he said. "Welcome to my home." He didn't wait for me and went in first. "You look tired. You have to rest, Monsieur Clatt. There," he extended his hand proudly.

The tiny bed made this room appear like an executive suite. But this bed was enticing, in spite of its dimensions.

"I bought a new mattress. Just for you," said Jean-Paul.

He didn't know how much I would appreciate any kind of mattress right now. It didn't matter how soft or hard, new or old it was, as long as it was flat. But something else bothered me enough to keep me from falling into bed immediately.

"How about my—" I paused. It was only visible as I stepped farther into the room. There was my black suitcase next to the bed. "How did it—?"

"Not to worry, Monsieur Clatt," my host said with the smile. "I told you that it is a small village, and everybody know everything. If I did not, I am telling you right now."

"But how did you know where I parked my car? And how did you get it from the car if I have the keys?" I tapped my jeans pocket just to make sure they were there.

"You are right, Monsieur Clatt." His face didn't reveal too much. "You parked your car in someone else's place, someone who reserved it a long time ago. There are families who rent all those spaces, and when they found out, it was easy to put everything together. All I had to do was ask."

"Still, I'm puzzled," I said, not quite sure how he was able to link the car to me, but it seemed irrelevant at that moment. The inviting milky bedding glowed in the dim room. Before I could ask another question, Jean-Paul turned toward the door.

"Good night, Monsieur Clatt," he said. "Sleep well, you have a lot to do—"

"Wait, wait!" I shouted. He paused and turned. I just couldn't leave this matter unresolved. "Just out of curiosity, how did you get inside the car? I thought I locked it."

My host's eyebrows narrowed. "Monsieur Clatt, you do not think I broke into the car?"

"No, not at all. I was just asking."

"That's the service I provide," he said. "I take care of my guests."

"Do you treat all your guests the same way?" I said.

Jean-Paul seemed to try to find the right words for his answer. He stood, silent for a moment, and then slowly spoke. "All who I had and all who arrive in the future. That is my duty, Monsieur Clatt." He wasn't smiling this time.

"Thank you," I said, afraid I had hurt his feelings.

"Not to worry, Monsieur Clatt," he said, his voice changing. "Before you sleep, you are hungry, yes? You must be hungry."

I hadn't eaten for a long time, but the truth was that I was more interested in sleeping than eating. I didn't feel the urge to do anything but meet the white linen, but a quick thought that maybe I should get something light before crashing ran through me in an instant. My host must've sensed it.

"How about orange juice and some fruit? It is light," he said.

I felt uneasiness in my chest. "Who are you? Are you some kind of a mind reader? A magician?"

"I am no magician, Monsieur Clatt. I am only a mere servant with a lot of practice. People always say what they want—they just don't know they say it."

"I didn't say anything."

"No, you did not, Monsieur Clatt, but I observed it," said my host with a smile.

I wasn't in the mood for any more of this conversation. "OK, then let's go with the orange juice and fruit. Should I go downstairs?"

"No, no," he waved his hands. "I bring it here. You rest, Monsieur Clatt. You need all the rest you can have," he said, and walked out of the room.

Chapter 13

A fat gloomy shadow covered the whole window when I woke up. Even if there were street lamps outside, they were not strong enough to break through the thick curtain of darkness. A bitter wind danced across the window panes in a mad ballet. Was it my imagination or had this gusty warrior blown the window open? Disoriented, I sat straight up in bed, searching for the old-fashioned clock I had seen before somewhere on the wall. I spotted it floating in the livid space beside me and stared intently at the glass covering its round face to find the slim pointing hands. It was just before five.

Morning? I asked myself, befogged about the time and place. I checked my wristwatch—it was closing at ten. Without thinking, half in sleep I adjusted it to the local time.

Nothing seemed real as I listened to the cold jeering quietness around me. I was almost sure that it was early morning. I had very vague, blurry memories of the previous day. I didn't remember what time I went to bed, but it seemed like I'd slept for a week. Not that I perceived myself rested or refreshed; but I owed my gratitude for those few hours that I didn't have to face the phantoms that had chased me for months. My head overflowed with questions, some of them so simple and prosaic, I was afraid I would never find the answers—others, as complicated as life itself. I wasn't sure if there was anyone who could help me find a solution. It felt as if no rescue was in sight. I was left all alone.

My brain received some steam from the hot shower. First of all, I thought, what am I doing here? Why did I decide to come, in spite of my doubts? Sally's last request couldn't be put aside and forgotten, that was unthinkable. I simply couldn't do that. That much was clear to me, for a change. But. There were so many "buts." Why now? She didn't explain anything, or leave any useful directions. Not a clue except the date: May 24. And even that was conveyed through Pete. I complied with her wish, and to make sure I was on time, I tried to come two days earlier. If not for my wayward suitcase, I would have been here yesterday. I steered away from thinking about last night's situation at the airport. I knew I shouldn't touch the subject for my mental heath sake. What is going on?

This was one of the times I absolutely failed to understand what Sally actually meant. There were times when Rosie...

Rosie! I have to call Pete.

Moments later, feeling my way along the wall, I raced downstairs, where I bumped into the reception desk. A single, diffused lamp had apparently been left on for the night. With a stifled curse, I turned around. The bar was deserted, bar stools evenly spaced along its length. No one was in sight, not even the crumpled little man.

The phone! I shook off the oppressive feeling of loneliness and leaned over the tiny countertop. Stretched over the reception desk with the receiver pressed to my ear, I dialed Pete, remembering to add a country code before the number. A daunting sound of deep dull silence echoed in my ear. What is wrong with this damn phone? I thought I shouted, and nervously looked around. I punched the buttons again, but there was no dial tone. Discouraged, I gave up, throwing the receiver back to its cradle. It bounced, and skittered along the glossy slab of the reception desk. I walked to the exit door. In anger, I pushed, and the glass door opened, unexpectedly soundless, revealing the unfamiliar world beyond.

The pre-dawn morning of southern France drew me out with a cold bluster of sea breeze. The air carried the fragrance of mermaids, and was as sharp as the trident of Neptune. I felt much better after its first reviving stab. The song of Sirens led me to the edge of the sea. I walked shoeless on the stinging sand where the dimmed Mediterranean Sea continued its work, transforming sharp, angular stones into harmless particles.

Few people were scattered on the beach, but more emerged from the darkness. Most of those already here were covered by warm blankets and listened to the numinous music of the waves, accompanying this monumental presentation by the greatest Showman of them all.

The sun teased at first, peering over the horizon to see if it had an audience, then slowly raised its bold head to peek from behind the curtain of cloud cover. But once it arose, there was no end to its staging. In one majestic pulse, it lit up the blanket of the sea. The waves began the illumination of colors with deep dark purple turning all the shades of bloody red, and ending with a festive orange and yellow.

Then in an instant, its radiant bows leapt from the horizon toward the shore. Surfing atop the foamy waves, they hit the land with lightning speed, and a violent, life-giving power. The sun didn't pause for its well-deserved standing ovation; it burst into its full glory as it rose higher and higher in the sky. In a matter of a few short minutes, the spectacular show was over, but the magic didn't end. There was always the promise of tomorrow's performance.

Astounded, I wished for an encore of the show, but only the golden sand remained as a witness. I turned back, letting the stream of warmth touch my shoulders, and strolled along the beach, lost in thoughts. There were many more people than I expected. In the daylight, I could see them lying in their nests in the sand. Some of them had fallen asleep; some gaped curiously into the sea, disappointed at the quick end of the spectacle. Their garb was similar to that of the people in the green Volkswagen I had followed yesterday. In the full glow of the morning light, I could easily admire their traditional style.

All the women wore long skirts in vivid bright colors and snow-white blouses topped with vests, which were embroidered with shining sequins; they danced barefoot on the sand as if trying to help the sun warm it up. Headbands couldn't prevent their gleaming raven hair from gliding on the breath of the sea.

The men wore black pants and white or ecru shirts, open to the waist and with sleeves rolled up. They treated their guitars and violins with gentle authority, giving birth to an unbelievable mixture of the sounds of the flamenco, rumba, and csardas. It was hard to tell who was singing. Starting with the solo far away, somewhere beyond the reach of my eyes, their voices grew stronger, forming duets, trios, quartets, until they peaked in the whole chorus, its dominant resonance covering the area, and then swinging away with the sea zephyr toward the village. I didn't understand anything, but it didn't matter; the eccentric melody—so pure and honest—was satisfying to me.

I was amazed when another display of light began. The dancing sun joined us by reflecting from their jewelry and lit the beach with golden sparkles. Both men and women had decorated their hands, wrists, and ankles with gold: earrings, bracelets, neck-laces, pendants, crosses, and rings. As if it wasn't enough, many wore thick golden chains around their necks. Nevertheless, it didn't interfere with their nimble moves, as they slipped from song to song without pause, each song different, new, and unforgettable.

The farther I walked along the beach toward the village, leaving the dancers behind, I encountered more and more of those who had missed the morning show, but were arriving to join this latest joyful celebration. I heard them talking with each other, shouting, and sometimes screaming at the careless children who approached too close to the water's edge. I couldn't recognize a single word, but it seemed that more than one language was being spoken. I desperately listened for some familiar sentences, phrases, or words, but I couldn't pick up anything spoken in English.

Before I entered the village, I stepped aside and watched in awe as the colorful flood of humanity took over the streets. I paused before mingling with the crowd, and then gently forced my way through, with little hope of getting directions back to the Hotel Europa. I took a long walk around the village, until I finally found the right street. In the middle of a wide curve, I spotted the familiar discolored canopy and the hotel's sign.

"Bonjour, Monsieur Clatt." I heard the voice of Jean-Paul just as I stepped over the threshold. "Good morning. Woke up early today, huh? Like a bird."

I wanted to say something but he kept going with the torrent of words. "You are not tired, Monsieur Clatt. Are you? Sacrébleu! You must be hungry, sit down." He pointed to one of the tables set up in the bar area. "The breakfast will be ready in no time for you." He rushed out from behind the reception desk, and held my elbow while pushing me in the direction of the table. He was like an old vinyl record that, when scratched, kept playing in a loop.

"I brought le fromage…cheese, fruits, and the tea last night but you were sleeping. I tried not to wake you. Did I? You sleep well?"

Finally, I managed to break free of his guiding hand and turned to face him.

"Thank you for everything, Jean-Paul," I said, subconsciously mimicking his style. "I slept well. And I'm sorry I couldn't wait for you, but sleep overwhelmed me. I don't know when I passed out."

"Tant pis! Not to worry, Monsieur Clatt." I was aware he was trying to take the lead again, but thought better of it as he confronted my look.

"Thank you for your breakfast invitation. I'm hungry after that morning walk, but first I have to call Pete. I didn't call last night, so if you'll excuse me, I have to—"

"No need to call him," he said, looking straight up at me.

"What?"

"We talk with Monsieur Roberts yesterday night. We talked long. I explained everything, and he is fine now."

"But why? How?" My host surprised me again. What was his role in this play? And Pete? He could easily call me here if he only wanted to. Whatever happens, no one will be able to explain.

Remember, Joe, you can understand only if you really want to. But you have to do it on your own. You will meet a lot of people who are ready to help you, but everything is in your hands, remember that. I recalled the quote from Sally's letter.

"Oh la la. Not to worry, Monsieur Clatt. Everything is fine. He know."

"But how is Rosie? Did he say anything?"

"She is fine, Monsieur Roberts said. Nothing happen since you—"

"I have to call. I'm sorry." I was determined to call Pete anyway. I couldn't figure out why Jean-Paul was handling everything for me. I didn't know why I wasn't able to make a phone call, but he could. And I didn't like the idea of being kept in the dark. "May I use your phone?" I tried to turn back toward the reception desk, but he grabbed my hand again.

"Par ici, s'il vous plait, please, Monsieur Clatt." He led me toward the dining room. "Now is too early; you call later. Let Pete sleep. He is tired too."

It seemed reasonable; my little host might be right. It was still early morning here, so with the seven hours difference, it made it the middle of the night back home. I calculated the time, and promised myself I would make the phone call around three in the afternoon. It would be eight in the morning in Fox River Valley Gardens, so Pete would be well awake at that time.

"You're right," I said. A smile formed on my host's face. "That's fine, I'll call him later. Now, what were you saying about breakfast being ready for me? If I may, of course?"

Barely visible from behind a wavy blue smog, there were a few people sitting at the short bar. They continued with their conversation after only a quick glance at Jean-Paul and me as we entered the room. Farther into the room, all four tables stood empty, but ready. My host let me choose the one I wanted. I moved across the room to the last table beside a small window. Without asking for permission, I grabbed the window's handle and tugged it. It was stuck but it gave after a few sharp pulls. Unfortunately, the light draft was too weak to clear all of the stale smoke inside this room, but at least my lungs didn't hurt that much. As silent as never, Jean-Paul wore his smile. I started to believe he was born with it.

"J'en suis desole. I know, I know," he said. "People know better no smoking here but they don't care. They smoke. But they my guests also."

"I really don't mind smoking," I said, which was true. "I smoked myself for many years, so I know how it is. I quit ten years ago. Well, maybe it was more than ten?" I looked at my host, but he wasn't interrupting me. That's something new. Even his conduct had changed, and I just realized what that was—he was not as hyper as he was a few minutes ago. A shadow of surprise stiffened him, and froze a smile to his face. Or was it a grimace? Did I say something wrong? Did I hurt his feelings? I just tried to open one stupid window— I started to worry, and tried to defend myself.

"It was just a little too—"

"Smoky?" he finished.

"Yeah, you are right. Too smoky," I said, and smiled.

Jean-Paul didn't say anything as he pulled out my chair, and his expression remained unchanged even after he seated me and disappeared through the bluish cloud by the bar.

The open window gave me a little breathing room, and by choosing that table, I picked—by accident—the best position to observe the whole dining room. As I waited, two separate families, both with children a few years younger than Rosie, took the two tables closest to mine. Their screaming kids joined forces to make sure their parents started their day with a loud kick. But the adults, drinking coffee and contemplating the breakfast menu, didn't pay attention to the little barbarians.

Trying to give the impression of being busy reflecting over the pure silverware and porcelain coffee cup placed on my table, I eavesdropped on their conversation. I was able to distinguish each word very well, but again they had no meaning to me. In contrast to most people I'd seen so far, this group wore contemporary casual clothes. But I was certain they weren't tourists. The modern clothes were more like a temporary disguise. Or was it my imagination?

A sudden roar jolted me from my lethargy. Within the bluish haze, a fight broke out between the men sitting by the bar. I had a good view of the whole spectacle even from one of the farthest rows from the scene.

They all were shouting simultaneously—about what I could only guess—their hands dangerously slapping the backs of the bar stools. The commotion was getting louder with every second; tightened fists flew in the air, but they were only feints. The men wheezed and whined, and shouted more sharp words to each other. Then, no fists this time, they only pointed fingers. I thought I might have caught a glimpse of them pointing in our direction.

I turned toward my neighbors; I wasn't sure if the gesture was directed toward me, or them. They seemed to be puzzled too. Their conversation had stopped, and all of them, including the children—trying not to appear too obvious—sneaked a quick look at me at the same moment I was checking them out.

I had a weird feeling crawling along my spine, a pins-and-needles tingle radiating from head to toe. A premonition of events over which I had no control gripped me. I didn't know whether to be afraid or fascinated. Nevertheless, this sensation kept me company until I spotted Jean-Paul darting out from the kitchen door. With only a few whispered commands, he ended their shouting match. Only then did the feeling gradually subside. After a moment, Jean-Paul returned to the kitchen.

He re-materialized a few minutes later, this time carrying a large waiter's tray on his shoulder. With the grace of a first-class juggler, Jean-Paul made it to my table. Precariously balancing the oversized platter with only one hand, he placed the tray on a portable stand, which he deftly unfolded with his free hand. In an instant, he filled the table with dishes of all kinds: fresh warm rolls, croissants, marmalade, honey, fruit jams, cheese, thin slices of salami, ham, and eggs.

The aromas rising from the table made it impossible to decide where to begin. The golden-brown coffee subdued me with its deep, provocative scent. I was spellbound by the beauty of the spread in front of me. I thought that even saints, if there were any,

wouldn't be able to resist the temptation. No invitation was necessary. I enjoyed my first bite of a warm, mouth-watering roll slath-
ered with homemade marmalade overflowing its edges. I expected
Jean-Paul to leave, but he didn't. Instead he stood on the opposite
side of the table, waiting for my response. I paused. Then mumbling
around a mouthful of food, I asked him to join me.

"Now, eat, Monsieur Clatt, you need the strength," he said,
sitting down across from me. Grabbing the coffee pot, he poured a
cup for each of us.

"Why do you think I need to be strong?" I said.

"Ça alors! Oh, I just said that. Everybody needs to be
strong," he said, and laughed. His face showed none of the earlier
tension; only his perfect teeth presented themselves prominently in
his smile.

Is this my imagination, again? I thought. I'm sure I'm missing something. "You're right, some more than others, but all of us
need our strength," I said.

"Well said, Monsieur Clatt, well said." He arched toward the
bar, and then turned back.

"So, tell me, what's the commotion in town about?" I asked,
my mouth full of melting rapture. I lowered my voice to a whisper,
not knowing why, afraid the families next to us could overhear my

remarks. "I don't think I have ever seen so many strange people in one place."

"Are they that strange to you?" he said.

"Can't quite say they're not. I don't think I have ever met—"

"I'm sure you did, Monsieur Clatt," he cut in. "You just didn't notice. Not paid attention enough."

"Maybe." I had to admit I'd never thought about it until then. "But do they speak English? I can't understand a word they say."

"Some of them do very well. Some are from America, some from England," said Jean-Paul, smiling all the while. "But you are correct; most...well they can't."

"What do they speak, then? It's not French, is it?"

"That is a mixture of many languages—they are Roms. They come from all over the world."

"Roms?" I said. "Ah, do you mean Gypsies?"

"Merde," said Jean-Paul, giving me a scolding look. "Oh, well, Monsieur Clatt. They don't like to be called Gypsies; they prefer Roms, or Gitanes."

"Gitanes sounds royal," I said, trying to wipe out the horrible impression I must've made on my host. "And the other names are fine too; it's just a matter of perception—"

"You didn't know?" He didn't let me finish.

"About what? Gitanes?" I said. "I don't think I've met one, but I have heard—"

"Not about them. I am sure, Monsieur Clatt, you have met more than one in your life. I meant you don't know what they are doing here?"

"You got me. Not a clue."

"Dieu la fete, Monsieur Clatt, what do they teach people over there?"

"Well…" I didn't know what to say.

"Do not be offended, Monsieur Clatt," said Jean-Paul, touching my hand, which was actually on a mission to grab another soft roll from the basket. "Not many people know about that. Every year on May 24, which is today, Roms have a huge holiday, and they pilgrimage from all over the world to observe it exactly where it happened."

"What happened?" I asked, hoping that I sounded curious enough.

"Their saint, a Saint Sara, disembarked two thousand years ago, and—"

"Wait, wait. Who is Sara?"

"Saint Sara is..." Jean-Paul closed his eyes. "Well, I will tell you in short. Saint Sara was a one of the people, a seven- or eight-year-old child who accompanied Mary Magdalene, and other Marys—"

"Mary Magdalene? Other Marys? What do you mean?" I didn't have to pretend anymore. I have always enjoyed legends.

"Three Marys and other apostles were forced to set sail in a rudderless boat because of the persecution after Christ's crucifixion. The boat drifted, and they landed here—"

I was certain he realized my questioning disbelief, but didn't say anything.

"Saint Sara is worshipped all over the world," Jean-Paul continued. "But in our village particularly. We are blessed. Her remains are kept in our church, though no one know exactly when, and how she died. Some say different things, but most agree that she was around forty when it happened."

"What happened?" I asked.

"'She died, unfortunately." He paused. "Oh, well. Getting back to us—long time ago Roms chose Saint Sara to be their patron."

"I haven't heard about any saint named Sara. But, well—" I said. "What do I know? A nice little army could be assembled from that group up there." I pointed my finger toward the ceiling.

"Regretfully," Jean-Paul said, in evident disregard of my digression, "Saint Sara is not recognized as a saint by the Catholics. But here, for Roms—for us—she is a saint, the holiest one, and here is her sanctuary. And today, it is her day, a feast of Saint Sara to observe the day of her arrival."

At first, my brain processed all the information with stoic calmness; then my thoughts began to oscillate, gaining speed, and spiraling out of control.

"Are you trying to tell me that I'm here in the middle of a Gypsy—sorry, Gitane—holiday? Are you trying to tell me it was my wife who made me come here just in time to celebrate the feast of Saint Sara?" I said. "Why?"

"That is how it seem to me, Monsieur Clatt," he said, smiling again.

"It doesn't make any sense. Why would she do that?" I was baffled.

"What did you say, Monsieur Clatt?" said Jean-Paul.

"I was asking you why," I said. "Obviously, you know more than I do. You found me, though I wasn't sure where was I going. You've talked with Pete, even when I tried to contact him and couldn't get a phone call through. You have never asked me why am I here, but from what I can tell, you already know, and are trying to hide it. Why did my wife request that I'd be here on May 24?"

"Monsieur Clatt, I do not—"

"Tell me!" I was determined to get something out of him right then. "No more games, no more magic tricks, just a straight simple answer."

"Monsieur Clatt, it is not like—"

"Tell me or...I am leaving," I bluffed. Jean-Paul opened his mouth—I got him. He finally would tell me everything. I saw it in his eyes. I was awaiting his revelation with intense attention when I overheard another loud altercation from the bar. Jean-Paul turned his head, and from my vantage point, I thought I saw a sign of reprieve on his face.

"Pardon, Monsieur Clatt," he said hastily, as he raced from my table.

Three men in their forties or fifties stood spaced evenly in front of the bar, staring through the cloud of smoke. All three of them were nearly the same height, a few inches shorter than me. Vivid silk shirts tucked into suit pants couldn't hide their growing paunches. Golden jewelry signified their authority, arousing the envy of others. With black hair and long thick mustaches, they resembled a mariachi trio. However, they didn't look like musicians—more like they were the paying spectators. And they seemed like the type that always took front row, reserved seats.

I was surprised to see an empty bar behind them; all of the previous occupants quietly stood next to the kitchen door. One-half of the swinging doors were ajar, and revealed a few pairs of eyes, searching for sensation. Not one of the trio paid any attention to onlookers. They watched Jean-Paul skillfully speed across the room to greet them. With hands gesturing wildly, they conferred by the bar. They were not arguing; from a distance, it seemed that they were trying to persuade him of something. After several minutes, they reached a resolution. They exchanged nods and smiles, and Jean-Paul rushed back to my table.

"Monsieur Clatt," he blurted out before coming to a stop. "I want to ask you question. Can I?"

"What?" I asked.

"Do you see these three gentlemen?" He nodded in their direction.

"It was very hard to miss them," I said. "Everyone but you ran away. I noticed they made quite an impression on you. Who are they?"

"Hmmm…How should I say it?" Jean-Paul fell silent for a moment. "The simplest way to put it is they are carefully chosen delegates to take part in today's affair."

"So?" I asked. "What has it got to do with me?"

"Monsieur Clatt, they came here to kindly ask you to speak with them," said Jean-Paul, his tone serious.

What is it now? I thought when I glanced toward the bar. The men waited patiently, their faces unperturbed.

"Me? Why?" I said.

Jean-Paul did not rush to answer. Though he tried to conceal it, I felt his demanding expression.

"They shall explain. It will be much better," he said.

"Fine," I said, surprising even myself. "Invite them in, but if you think I'll let you off the hook that easily, without answering my questions, you're mistaken."

"What question, Monsieur Clatt?"

"Come on, you know what I'm talking about."

"Oh, that," he said as he smiled. "Monsieur Clatt, let me tell you this. There are some questions that can be answered only by the one who ask them...” His eyes revealed nothing. “Now let me get them—they are really important, you know,” he said, and he ran back toward the bar. As if on cue, a tall, burly woman turned up next to me and, without sparing a gaze, swept my table clean.

The black-haired, nearly indistinguishable triplets approached with Jean-Paul walking a few steps behind them. They were no different from the other Roms I’d seen so far, except maybe their aura of self-confidence—it seemed much thicker. Their hands extended nearly simultaneously to grasp the chair backs. Each one wore a bulky golden ring on his right-hand ring finger. Intrigued by the size of the rings, I tried to get a better look, but they vanished beneath the table the moment the men sat down.

With his head bowed, Jean-Paul said, “Monsieur Clatt, I was asked by these fine gentlemen to help them with the translation; their knowledge of English, how should I say it—” He paused. “Well, let me tell you that my services will be in need. Do you mind?”

“Of course not. That’s fine,” I said, intrigued a little. I have shared tables with many different people, but it was one of the few times someone had made me feel so important.

“Very well, then,” he said.

The three men sat quietly, and I wondered if they truly didn't know English, or if this was just another game I was forced to play.

"As I already mentioned," Jean-Paul motioned in their direction. "Here are three of the four delegates necessary to provide the most important task for today's Saint Sara's procession." He nodded toward them. "Every year on the day of the Saint Sara feast, there is a parade that takes a statue of Saint Sara from her shrine to the sea, and then back to the church, where it rests in peace, to memorialize her holy arrival."

If I said I wasn't at least a little interested, I'd be lying. I couldn't wait to see where this was leading. I couldn't think of any relation between Saint Sara, Sally, and me, but nevertheless it was something to keep me busy while searching for the real reason I was here in France.

"You see, Monsieur Clatt," Jean-Paul continued, "we have a problem this year."

His prolonged pause forced me to ask, "What kind of problem?"

"There are four people needed to carry the statue. Those people are carefully chosen, and it is a great honor for them to be selected for this task." He paused again. The three chosen ones said nothing, so I also decided to withdraw all my questions for the moment.

"This year everything is ready, almost," Jean-Paul continued. "Almost, because there was an accident, an unfortunate illness of one of the delegates." His eyes quickly moved across my face. "The fourth person chosen to carry the statue can't provide the service anymore."

"OK, I'm aware of the situation now," I said, slowly moving my eyes from Jean-Paul to those three men. "But what has it got to do with me?"

"You see, Monsieur Clatt," said Jean-Paul, exhaling loudly. "All the so-called kings of the Roma families present in our village gathered today and decided to kindly request your assistance. They would like you to help them."

"Help?" I looked up at those unfamiliar men at my table. Immobile as monuments, they continued to survey me intently. Their voiceless, penetrating question hung in the tranquil air of the dining room. Just then, I was more than certain they could understand every single word of our conversation, but I couldn't figure out why they hadn't spoken.

"I have a question, if I may?" I said slowly.

"Yes, Monsieur Clatt," said Jean-Paul.

"Why didn't they ask for help from anyone from their...families?"

"That is a very good question, indeed," he said, taking his eyes off me.

For a moment, they all whispered, conferring in a language I, of course, wasn't familiar with. After a short time, Jean-Paul used English again.

"The answer is a little complicated, Monsieur Clatt," he said. "There is a little-known belief that, if one of the chosen cannot carry out his duties because of death or illness, there has to be another person selected from outside the families who already have had their delegates."

"OK, that explains one thing," I said. "But there are thousands of people here, and I am sure they could easily find someone who doesn't belong to their families. So why me?"

I sat unmoving, listening to the chatter for several minutes before Jean-Paul spoke to me again.

"Monsieur Clatt, my guests here," he pointed his palm toward the delegates, "...would like to ask you for help because of what happened in the morning."

"This morning? It's still morning, as far as I know. What happened to earn me their invitation?"

"I will try to explain it, Monsieur Clatt—" Jean-Paul said after another hushed conversation with the trio.

"That would be great, because I'm a little confused here."

"They have seen you on the beach in the early morning, at the sunrise," said Jean-Paul.

"So what? Why's that so special? I saw many other people too. Quite a crowd gathered on the beach, to be honest. Why didn't they choose one of them?"

"Yes…they have seen them too—"

"So?"

"But you were the only one who was waiting," said Jean-Paul.

"Waiting?"

"Yes, waiting. Everyone else just watched; you were the one who witnessed—"

"I didn't see anything more than the others," I cut in quickly.

"You did, Monsieur Clatt, You just didn't realize it," he said, glancing at those three men at our table. "Once they set their eyes on you over there, they already knew you were the one. There was no doubt about that."

"About what?" I said. "There is no doubt about what?" I repeated the question impatiently, but Jean-Paul seemed not to be listening.

The situation was getting out of hand. I thought about all of those odd circumstances associated with this whole trip, about those weird feelings I'd had more often than not ever since I'd arrived. In the beginning, I blamed jet lag, the long flight, my sleepless nights before departure—but now, it was getting too bizarre for me. Not only did I not know why I was here, I had experienced hallucinations, and, a minute ago, I was asked to be one of the chosen ones. Chosen to carry a statue of a saint, who in truth wasn't a saint, but Gypsies—or I should've said Roms—believe is one. Finally I have been selected to be at the center of attention in the Saint Sara feast by three men from out of nowhere.

Why have they asked me out of so many people? And I am not even a Gypsy. No one from my family had any Gypsy roots. I searched deep back in my memory. No—there was no Gypsy blood, as far as I knew.

I sensed a curious tension building in the room. Exchanging poorly concealed fleeting looks, the three Roms patiently waited as I absorbed all the information. I hadn't made my decision yet. Impulsively I wanted to say no—I didn't think that the whole show with the procession would bring me any closer to finding the answers to my questions. But seeing this situation from a different perspective, I didn't have any promising options open to me. I was there without any direction or help except Jean-Paul, who was apparently withholding more than a little. And I was convinced he wouldn't disclose more than he thought necessary. *You will meet a lot of people who are ready to help you, but everything is in your hands, remember that.* Sally's words worked their magic. Anyway, this is better than nothing, I concluded.

I looked up at the delegates and Jean-Paul. I was sure they assumed from the beginning what my answer would be, but they probably didn't anticipate how long it would take to get the right one from me. They waited in the long silence, and I finally decided to get it over with.

"Would you please answer for me, Jean-Paul?" I asked him, as I avoided looking at those three men.

"Of course, Monsieur Clatt." His voice did not have its usual confident timbre.

"Would you tell these gentlemen that I am deeply honored, and very thankful for their invitation to carry out such a noble duty, and to help them celebrate their holiday, and—"

"Monsieur Clatt, before—" I thought I heard a trace of panic in Jean-Paul's voice.

"—And I gratefully accept. I am really deeply honored. Please tell them that I will do whatever I can to help. I just hope that I will not disappoint."

It was the biggest smile out of all the smiles Jean-Paul had given me so far, and there was a little commotion on the other side of the table as well. Jean-Paul quickly shouted some words in their direction, and they finally broke their stillness and gave a light cheer. They rose from their chairs simultaneously and shook my hand one by one, making me a little uncomfortable by bowing their heads in respect. I replied in kind to each of them. They left the room, relaxed, talking, and laughing softly. Suddenly, one of them turned back. The whole room was empty except for us, as both families previously occupying other tables had gone too.

"Thank you for your help, Monsieur Clatt. We are really looking forward to seeing you this afternoon."

I knew it! That was my first thought. I knew you could speak English, you— I wanted to say something to him, but before I could disgrace myself, he was out the door with the other two.

"What was it about?" I asked Jean-Paul when they were gone.

"Monsieur Clatt," he started with that prolonged tone he used when he was trying to say not more than he should.

"Remember, you owe me one," I said, and I laughed. Without any reasonable explanation, at that moment I couldn't care less about what he was, or wasn't, going to tell me.

He laughed with me and said. "There are a few things that need to be prepared. You have to get ready for this afternoon."

Chapter 14

All the events so far were as unanticipated and astounding, as I would never be able to imagine such, even in the most bizarre dreams. I didn't have a chance to reason about what I was getting myself into; now it was a little too late. Jean-Paul left me to myself.

Just thinking about the preparations mentioned by Jean-Paul made me shudder. The whole idea was a bit out of the ordinary, and I didn't feel comfortable at all. On the other hand, I was pleased to have been chosen as a replacement for one of the most important participants of this afternoon's procession. Saint Sara never meant anything to me before; she didn't now, either. I didn't even know about her existence until this morning, but being selected out of so many people gathered there—

But wait! Something's wrong here. Why me? Why? They had so many people to choose from, their own kind. They said they saw me waiting. Waiting? What was that supposed to mean? Is this a coincidence or—

I went up to my room, lay down on the bed, and tried to clear my mind. There wasn't anything more relaxing, more calming for me than to just think about nothing.

My hand sought out the remote control on the nightstand, but only then, I found out that there was no remote because there was no TV in the room. It didn't matter—I wouldn't be able to absorb anything anyway, but for a moment I felt a touch of self-pity at being stuck without a television. Not that I didn't have enough odd things happening to me already, but I just needed a momentary diversion.

The only problem for me was a sudden wild thought. I tried to force it out, but it just wouldn't go away. I was afraid this was only the beginning, and there was much more to come. I wasn't sure what or when, but I knew this was not the end. I still couldn't explain how all of this was related to Sally's last request, even when I put my best effort into it. It just didn't click with anything; nothing matched.

I'll have to wait and see. Just wait and see. I tried to talk myself into this unfamiliar approach, but instinctively I was preparing myself for the unknown.

I knew the questions would come again, and they did as expected. I was lying down when they crept up, filling my head with a rough uncontrollable fire. I tried to hold them on a leash as long as possible, but they exploited one slight moment of inattention. Was everything set up by...whom? Pete? Did he prepare everything so it appeared like that? There were too many coincidences. But how? And why? What am I missing?

Everything, so far, pointed in Pete's direction. He planned the whole trip since day one. Lost luggage? OK, that was just an accident; I can swallow that. But then how did the little French chameleon locate me on the streets of the village even though he had never met me before? How did he know I was the one he was looking for? He offered simple explanations, but somehow they sounded too simple. Then, Jean-Paul's conversations with Pete—he didn't let me call him! And even if I tried without his knowledge, I didn't get through. And the last thing was this whole procession affair. Is this a setup? If not, then what? What is going on? Should I just leave this strange place and run, run to...Rosie? ...Rosie will be fine. She will need a lot of help and attention...

I jumped out of bed—this was too much. I intended to go downstairs and call Pete immediately, determined to straighten things out with him right then. No more playing around, no more surprises, and no more weird twists of fate—I had a right to know. But after a few steps, I abruptly stopped. The letter. There was no possible way that Pete could falsify Sally's letter to me. There was no question about that. I was certain he didn't possess the audacity to pull a stunt like that; he was way too honest. Anyway, Sally's handwriting couldn't be forged. I had no doubt—she wrote the letter. But if Sally really wanted me to come here, why had she never mentioned it before? Why wouldn't she give me some hint, a little clue as to what it was about? During all of our life together, I never doubted her, not once, always trusting her in whatever situation we were in. I was always proud to think that there were no secrets between us. In reality, it wasn't the case, and it was dreadfully hard for me to admit I was mistaken.

Why did she send me to this unknown place, precisely defining the day I should be here? Why not some other day? Any day of the year seemed as good as today to me, so why the schedule? Requesting me to be here on the day of the feast of Saint Sara, who was, in fact, not a saint at all?

Sally, a Catholic, singled out the day when commemoration of this person, who was not even recognized as a Catholic saint, takes place. And then, most important, the Roms, the people who have chosen Saint Sara as their patron, just selected me out of the thousands of people present, to carry Saint Sara's statue this afternoon? And I wasn't a Gypsy. Not even close, not at all, no connection whatsoever. Not to the Roms, nor to the French—there was nothing I could find in common with either of them. It doesn't make any sense! Or does it? If it does, then—

I sat down back on the bed. Only my thoughts of Sally and her mysterious, baffling request kept me from running out of here. If I learned one thing from her, it was to trust her. And I did in spite of the secrets she left behind. I didn't know how much time had passed when I heard knocking on my door.

"Come on in," I shouted from the edge of the bed.

Jean-Paul came in silently, his face colorless and gaunt. No attempt at idle conversation this time. Instead, his eyes flicked through the room, then rested on me, and he asked, "Are you ready, Monsieur Clatt?"

"I don't know. I think I am."

"How should I say it? Sacrébleu!" He paused, his brow furrowed in thought. "Not to worry, Monsieur Clatt. Let the things go their own way. Do not fight the fate, Monsieur Clatt. It is a tough contest—nobody won it yet."

"Nobody won?" I said. "You're probably right. There is little I can do right now, is there?"

"If I may give you my advice—just let it go, Monsieur Clatt. The past is gone. Embrace the future; you never know what it could bring. Don't try to control it; it is not possible. Just let it take a path on its own." Jean-Paul didn't give me a chance to answer. "Would you mind if we change your wardrobe a little later?" He paused. "We have to make you look noble, for it's a honor to carry the statue of Saint Sara. I—"

"I don't have any formal clothing. I came just for a few days, so—"

"Not to worry, please, Monsieur Clatt," he said. "Not to worry. Where we are going, we do not have to worry about such trivial things. Your friends or, should I say, your new family, they will provide everything that will be needed."

My new family? That's going a little too fast—I had just met them. I was tempted to say something, but I decided to let this comment slide.

Jean-Paul walked up to the door, and opened it. "After you, Monsieur Clatt."

We forged our way through the crowd that filled the center of the village all the way down to the sea. Then we took a walkway along the shore leading away from town. We approached the same large open field where I had left my Renault yesterday.

I followed Jean-Paul who navigated deep inside the maze. An oasis of large trees, overgrown with bushes, exposed themselves proudly in a semicircle that formed a natural fence—a living curtain of camouflage. As I walked out from around the trees, I couldn't stop pinching myself. If not for Jean-Paul's nimble steps ahead of me, I would swear I was dreaming. It was a view taken directly from the fairy tales of my childhood. Rainbow-painted wagons, set up in a traditional circle, dominated the whole clearing. Through the buzzing noise of the field of pilgrims, I overheard the faint snorts of horses. After a few more steps toward the wagons, the scent of horse sweat, combined with the smell of soggy hay, was unmistakable.

Through a gap between the wagons, we entered a loop of colorful carts and left the present behind us. There were a few people strewn around the central fire hole. All of them turned their heads in our direction. Their intrigued stares made me apprehensive, but Jean-Paul kept going, shouting out shrill words that had no meaning to me.

"Where are we?" I whispered.

"Not to worry, Monsieur Clatt," said Jean-Paul, walking toward one of the wagons parked on the opposite side of the fire hole. "Let's go. They are waiting for us."

Expressionless Roms followed our every move as we neared the door. While we were passing them by, Jean-Paul acknowledged each one with a slight bow of his head. None of them moved, but I could feel their eyes on my back. The wooden door emitted a loud shriek when someone swung it open from the inside. A man with a sharply trimmed mustache waved his hand, and mutely invited us inside. He let us in, and closed the door behind us.

The interior of the wagon seemed much bigger than I expected. Except for three small sofas, there was not a piece of furniture inside. The heavy green curtains covered the windows on each of the two longer walls. There was no other light except the diffused rays that smuggled themselves inside through the vertical cracks where two curtains met.

I didn't identify them right away. Only after Jean-Paul started to give honor to each of them, one by one, was I sure that these three Roms sitting on the sofa were the same men I met earlier in Hotel Europa. But I noticed someone else inside too. He stood farther inside the room in a deep blind corner, untouched by light.

He didn't say a word. Neither did I. The three Roms sat down, again, but this time they squeezed themselves into only one couch, leaving the other two vacant.

"Sit down, Monsieur Clatt," said Jean-Paul. "Relax, please; almost everything is ready."

"What is ready?" I said.

"Your attire for tonight." He pointed across toward the Roms. "They have prepared everything. Only minor alteration will be done. The tailor is waiting." He waved his hand. "If necessary, of course."

"My what?"

"It's just for this afternoon. Nothing fancy, but, as you said, you don't have much choice in your wardrobe. It's just nice pants and a shirt. Not really a costume, just a proper outfit for the occasion."

"Oh, well," I said. "Am I going to be just like them?"

"Kind of, Monsieur Clatt," said Jean-Paul, flashing another perfect smile at me.

I was wordless; logical thinking went astray. The whole ceremony, and all those steps that led to it, were nothing major. I could play along as I promised, but first I had to get an answer from Jean-

Paul. This one particular question had been bothering me since this morning, and I had to get him to answer it.

"Do they speak any English?" I asked, trying to point in the direction of the Roms with my eyeballs.

"Who?" Jean-Paul seemed to be surprised. "Ah, them?" He smiled. "Not at all. One is German, one Romanian, and one French. They can communicate in German pretty well, and of course, they speak Gypsy, but not English. I'm sorry."

"So, why did he," I impolitely pointed at the man in the middle, and I hoped he was the right one, "use English when—"

"Oh, that?" Jean-Paul smiled. "I just taught him a few words, that's all."

I remained unconvinced. "So how am I going to be any help to them? I won't be able to understand anything they say. And I assume you won't be there to help me, will you?"

"Not to worry, Monsieur Clatt. It won't be necessary. You don't need me there. Just watch whatever they are doing, and do the same. It won't be that hard."

Jean-Paul answered the delegates' questions, and when they paused, I had a chance to ask him a couple more myself.

"Are you sure I can make it?"

"Mon Dieu. Yes, Monsieur Clatt," he said. "Anyway, you will be close together. You all will be holding the statue, so just imitate them—it will not be hard, I promise. After you put the statue back, you can do as you please. You can mingle with the crowd for a while, enjoy, and relax. I'll be waiting for you, but don't hurry; take your time. Oh…and the attire is yours. Treat it as our gift, please."

"Are you going to be there?" I asked.

"I'm sure I will. I don't know exactly where yet. There will be so many people. I doubt you'll find me. Stay close to them, and once you get to the church, everything will be OK."

"But—" I spotted one of the three Roms fidgeting.

"I'm sorry, Monsieur Clatt." Jean-Paul took it as a sign. "We have to move. Please try this on."

Jean-Paul said something in the language of the Roms, and the tailor came out with a richly frilled white silk shirt and a pair of granite-black slacks.

"Try it on, please," repeated Jean-Paul.

"Well…fine." I took the clothes, and saw that they were identical to those worn by the three Roms. But their matching shoes bothered me a little. I looked down at my own sneakers, and before I raised the question, Jean-Paul reassured me.

"Not to worry about the shoes, Monsieur Clatt. You can find your size over there." He pointed toward the dark corner of the room, where the tailor had been standing.

"There are boxes of shoes. I am sure you will find a pair that will fit. Put everything on, and then come over here." He pushed me gently toward the other side of the room.

The sun had followed more than half of its daily routine, when we finally came out of the wagon. Like four tin soldiers, we wore identical outfits. Ready for the parade, we proudly marched along the sea toward the center of the village. The vibrant, multi-hued, tuneful crowd parted, and the three Roms wordlessly led the way while I followed a few steps behind, heeding Jean-Paul's words of advice. In the meantime, Jean-Paul had disappeared without warning, and I was left on my own.

The whole village pulsed with life. Everyone there joined us in our walk. The violins and guitars grew louder with each step, enhancing the power of the unfamiliar lyrics and carrying their heartwarming essence on a gentle wind. We stopped just once, by the steps leading to the Church of the Three Saints, which was located on the largest of the village squares. I remembered passing it several times yesterday while dashing around in search of the hotel.

But it was just one of the many buildings I ignored then. I didn't know then that its immense stone walls guarded a precious relic.

A Catholic Church? Didn't Jean-Paul tell me that Sara wasn't recognized as a saint? So what were we doing here?

I didn't have more time to think about that, and no one in particular to ask. We entered through the massive wooden gate. A chilly blow of mystery welcomed us into the dim main nave, sheltered by an enormous vaulted ceiling; it demanded our absolute attention. As our eyes adjusted to the light, we advanced slowly toward the stairs, located beside the main altar. Rows of pilgrims filled the church, and waited for our arrival.

They stepped aside, opening a path down the aching wooden staircase to the underground crypt. Its whitewashed concrete walls supported the ceiling, covered by a thick layer of aged silt, which hung just few inches above my head. An ancient wooden altar came into sight as we stepped into the crypt, illuminated by hundreds of tall immaculate candles that arose from rectangular stands hugging the walls. The shadows of the three crosses, projected on the wall, partially concealed a lifelike figure of Saint Sara, which stood upon a black rock by the small altar.

A procession of people moved forward, long candles in their hands. But the altar was not the focus of their affection. They were approaching the statue of Saint Sara, some awkwardly leaving cautious kisses on her mahogany cheek or hand, others giving timid touches, as though one wrong move might spoil this moment. A few added their pleading requests to the wooden monument by her side, which held a mound of letters.

The small crutches and metal braces placed behind her bore witness to miraculous answers. From under the shadow of her crown, shy eyes appeared to sow blessings through the crowd, missing no one. Multiple layers of freshly ironed capes draped her shoulders in colors of blue, rose, and white. Shiny golden necklaces, cut with sparkling jewels, and a bouquet of fresh flowers in her hands were merely decorative accents; she has been magnificent just by herself. I knew she observed us patiently, embarrassed by the lavish attention, yet ready for her ceremony. I couldn't take my eyes off her.

An unexplainable feeling of happiness welled up within me, and I shared a sacred union with all those around us, as we raised her, and headed toward the stairs. My body shook, making my hands slip on the wooden pole. I held on, but after a few steps, the pole left blisters on my palms. I realized that carrying her all the way to the shore and back wouldn't be an easy duty. But at the same time, I felt I must keep going, no matter what the cost. Nothing was more important to me than carrying Saint Sara.

A vision of Rosie and Sally unexpectedly crossed in front of my eyes, but it was soothed immediately by the soft touch of one of Saint Sara's capes as a breeze brushed it over my hand. I felt too safe with her to be afraid of anything. We briefly stopped at the ground level, in the nave, and, copying my partners, I bowed my head toward the main altar.

At the first indication of our appearance through the church's gate, the thunderous cry from a thousand throats roared above the square, shouting repeatedly, "Vive, Sainte Sara!"

Joining the clamorous sound of the pulsating hearts of the church bells, the fiddlers and guitarists plucked at their strings and dozens of other instruments, as the chant "Vive, Sainte Sara! Vive, Sainte Sara!" grew louder and louder with every second. Gardians astride white horses held medieval wooden lances, which once would have guarded Saint Sara, and they semi-productively tried to clear the way for us.

Slowly, we proceeded through the zigzagging streets toward the sea. I had the impression that even more people joined our procession as we slowly moved forward, but I hadn't expected such a vast gathering on the sandy shore. Witnesses covered the beach, jockeying for the best positions. Some were clever enough to jump into the water and wait for us there. A few ignored the Gardians and their horses, and stood in our way as if the sand had glued their feet in place and would not allow them to move aside. Only their wet eyes revealed the truth.

A peppery whiff filled the air. Careful not to submerge the precious Saint Sara in the salty water, we went in and stopped just a few yards from the shoreline. The Gardians let their horses wade in a circle around us, our bodies chilled by the calm sea, which seemed to glow, embracing us. The combination of the beach symphony and the consoling hum of the gentle waves drifted around us.

A single rifle shot cracked, breaking the performance for mere seconds. I noticed everybody moving, and glanced at my partners. Silently they nodded their heads toward the land. The sound of countless harmonies flew over us, carried by the gentle waft. Holding Saint Sara in our extended arms, we took short but certain steps and gradually rose from the sea. A thunder of ecstasy flashed through the air once we stepped onto the beach with a triumphant Saint Sara gazing over the crowd. With the joyous triumph echoing around us, the procession started again.

The Gardians led the way back to the church, accompanied by the myriad tones and rhythms. As the music mixed and mingled, no heart was left untouched. An unfamiliar force transformed everything. The sputtering of the lit candles, the tang of liquid wax absorbed us all, creating a sanctuary, which sheltered us from the outside world.

We carried Saint Sara down into the crypt, and gently placed her next to the altar where a pale spot, bordered by the marks of thousands of teardrops, indicated her home. It seemed my job was finished, and I slowly examined my surroundings in awe. I never thought I would be so proud of myself because I helped to carry the statue of a saint, not to mention, a saint I had never heard of before this morning. But I was. I was proud and happy, willing to do it all over again, if needed.

My three Roma partners approached me and patted my back as we exchanged smiles. They said something I didn't get. And then they ushered me to the door. It was time to go. My intuition was informing me they would try to ask me to join them, but I needed to be left alone.

Quickly I attempted to immerse myself in the swarm outside the church. But my three friends tugged at my arm in an attempt to take me with them. I just shook their hands.

"I'm sorry," I said as politely as I could. "And thanks for everything. I'll just take a walk."

They stood curiously next to me; I thought they got a wrong idea, and assumed I was agreeing to join them. They talked together momentarily, and then one of them said, "It was a honor to meet you, Monsieur Clatt."

What was that baloney about them not being able to speak English? I thought. This wasn't just a memorized sentence.

"I'm really so—" I said, but they were no longer standing beside me—gone, as the nameless crowd tucked me in its blissful arms.

Singers and dancers filled every street as I swam with the unstoppable current of spectators and performers. The village, pulsing with its own rhythm, was a separate living organism, suspended in its own microcosm, unaware of anything outside its own borders.

I needed time to think. I needed to get to the shore again, to see its supernatural beauty lying down to sleep with only the moon shadows as a blanket. I wanted to sit and listen to the last call of the day. Making my way through the stream of bodies was tricky, and it was even more difficult with no Gardians around to clear the way. After a lot of careful twisting and turning, I somehow made it to the edge of the sand in one piece. A clamorous crowd claimed the beach too. The crystals of sand reflected the chorus of the light and music far away into the indigo water. In return, the calm pane of the Mediterranean Sea shot it back to the shore, a sweet echo of the celebration—a past, which had been called a present just seconds ago.

Determined to gather my thoughts in a more secluded place, I strolled along the waterline, farther from the festivities on the beach. I took my shoes off and walked slowly, seeking peace with the unpredictable mother of life. The crowds gradually grew thinner, but I had to walk for a long time to find myself quietly alone. What do you want, Sally? I can't stay and wait, when Rosie— I didn't allow myself to finish the thought. I needed help, any kind of help, for that matter.

The silver joker showed its bold head for a moment, then hid himself behind the cover of scattered clouds. Guided by the fragments of voices and music at my back, I walked with my ankles submersed in the chilly water—as if that would change something. After more than fifty yards of my lonely march, the darkness that accompanied me felt so close, I was sure I could touch it just by extending my hand. The music, the voices were gone; only the calm susurrus of the sea reminded me where I was.

I put my shoes back on, and for a moment contemplated the return to the Hotel Europa. The familiar spice of sea salt mixed with strong white pepper provoked my senses, waking me from my reverie. Its strength increased with every step I took and finally, I had to stop, disoriented. I squatted as if that would help me to locate its source. When I got up, and raised my head, my legs suddenly refused to move even an inch farther, and the circulation in my body abruptly clogged.

Not more than a dozen feet ahead on the black canvas of the night, a deeper shadow rose from the water, though I couldn't tell what it was. A slow, steady heartbeat of the sea filled the air around me. The scent was gone in an instant as if the wind decided to skip the party and took it away. My scream for help, if I had been able to produce one, wouldn't have been heard until the sunrise. By then, it probably would be too late anyway. I considered my options, and with my heart shrunk to the size of a cherry, I decided to check on whatever had settled on the sand.

With my hands extended in front of me like a shield, I slowly walked in the direction of the object. As I approached, it gradually revealed its true shape. By the time I could almost touch it, I made out it was an askew beached boat. As the late evening draft had gone, the sound of faint waves breaking on the boat's hull was all I could hear. I ignored the cold water soaking my legs as I circled the boat. Made out of battered pieces of wood, it was six to eight feet wide and not longer than thirty feet. I searched for survivors of the unexpected collision with solid ground.

While I moved along the sides, a shy, nearly undetectable flame of light wavered in the middle of the boat. It seemed to be covered by a shade, which did not let the full strength of its light out. Feeling along the salt-bitten rail, I leaned over to peer inside. The light was gone. Dark and empty as half of an open walnut, the rough deck was clear. Even a ship's mast, if ever there had been one, was missing. There was no sign of any motor in the back, and no place for it. Muscle power must have propelled this boat, but I could locate neither rudder nor oars. I couldn't find anything. There was nothing useful to push the boat through the waves.

I scanned the boat for yet another time, swiveling my head around, but discovered nothing new. The light I thought I had seen moments ago must have been an illusion. But when I turned my head back toward the boat, I jerked in surprise and let go of the rim. I tumbled down and sank into the sea with a sizable splash. I wasn't sure if I screamed. When I recouped and subdued my desire to run away, I pulled myself up on the boat's edge again.

They were still there. A group of people sat on the boat's deck around a small lantern. At least a dozen people wore brown or gray mantles, their heads covered, and their large shapes surrounded a smaller figure tucked between two of them. They all sat quietly, concerned only with their tiny light.

Ignoring my presence on the edge of the boat, a few of the passengers stood up and disembarked into the shallow water on the opposite side. The others moved right after, taking turns, and only then was I able to catch a glimpse of one face. I had seen him before; there was no way I would ever forget him. Even the wrap above his head was no disguise. The crooked mouth and the smeared hair of the man from the Marseille airport were not easy to forget. Simultaneously the extraordinary trace of pepper dust on the salty water floated around me again. I would be lying if I said I didn't panic at that moment. But panic turned to shock, its intensity unbearable, and just a heartbeat from cardiac arrest.

It seemed there was one last person in the boat, waiting to be helped ashore. The dim glow of the lantern couldn't penetrate the curtain of the night more than a couple of feet, so only after a slight movement on the boat's deck, I saw the small shape of a child, almost indistinguishable from the adult whose arms embraced it. After only a second, they again existed as one.

I waited in the shadow of the night for the next few minutes, with only the whisper of waves breaking on the tired hull as a witness. I observed the child move first, guided by the adult toward the rim where a pair of helping hands waited to carry it ashore. Baffled, it turned around and faced me instead. Although the child was not more than two feet from me, I couldn't see its face, hidden under the oversized cloth hung over its head. The hair was cut short and it was all I could see; even the eyes were hidden deep inside the cover. After a split second, the child turned around again and disappeared into the arms of someone on the other side of the boat.

I saw the caretaker of the child grabbing the lamp and awkwardly trying to cross over the edge. I held my position, hanging on with my bottom half plunged in the cold salty water on the seaward end of the boat. Using just my arms to support myself, I didn't dare move while the scene unfolded. My body screamed for a rest, and I was quite ready to let go and lay down on the sand, when the lantern's last breath illuminated a face on the opposite side of the boat. At first, it was just a face. But then it struck me just below my rib cage. The kid's guardian veil had fallen down uncovering wine colored hair, curled by the salt and wind. Tremendous pain squeezed my soul as I slipped off the boat into the water, and ran ashore.

I found her carefully stepping through the water, her hand held by an unrecognizable supporter. Instinctively, I came closer, my eyes glued to her face. The helper was gone, and she was on the sand by herself. The lantern was lit again as she held it up, and started to walk in my direction. Her hair became more vivid with every step, while the trembling light cast puzzling shadows on her face. There was no sign of any other passenger around, but I didn't care. They must have blended with the dimness covering the rest of the beach. Even the sea's slight waves calmed, flattened by the weight of the night's thick shroud.

I should have gone back to see Jean-Paul instead of walking on the beach. It probably would have been smarter, I thought, but I held my ground and waited.

At first, I was scared, ready to run for help, but not able to move. When my panic reached its peak, a feeling of the most unbelievable calmness curled around me. One could anticipate this kind of peace only with death. At that moment, in front of my doubting eyes stood someone I never expected to see again—my wife.

Sally? I was confused. That woman certainly looks like my wife, almost exactly like her but— it is late at night, almost no lights around, only the small lantern. I am tired, I can't see very well. No, it's not her. How could it be anyway? Sally is…

As if she could read my thoughts, that…woman approached me, moving the lamp to her side. Her closeness caused my reservations to wane. I quickly noticed her green tunic beneath the red woolen cloak, the white veil rested on her shoulders. Her fawn leather sandals were soaked. It was the view of her feet that shocked me the most—they were an exact cast of my wife's. I remembered them too well. As a last resort to preserve my rationality, I glanced at her right hand. The lantern's poor light was enough to dispel doubt. Right between her thumb and index finger, a diamond-shaped freckle perfectly matched Sally's. If not for the bizarre circumstances on the beach, I would swear she was my wife, and I would fight anyone bold enough to contradict me. I couldn't take it any longer. My heart leaped and I rushed at her with my arms extended, and shouted, "Sally! Sally!"

She acted as if she expected my outburst. By simply raising her free hand in unmistakable authority, she stopped me short of touching her. But she didn't stop me from whispering her name over and over again.

Instead of an answer, she placed her finger on her round mouth, hushing me like a little child, her voice bringing soft, sweet memories. When I was able to give my attention to the words she was saying, I realized she was speaking in a language I hadn't heard before. Even here in France, where I had encountered a multitude of different tongues, this was a new one. There was something extraordinary in the melody of her voice. I couldn't decide if it was an accent, or a slight coarseness, but it didn't matter. I half closed my eyes, and didn't pay attention to the words being spoken; I just listened to the familiar music of her intonation. I couldn't be wrong—it was Sally's voice—the same tone and pitch. She even moved her lips the same when she spoke, twitching them subtly after each finished the sentence.

I thought I was crazy. No, I didn't think—I was certain.

I started to call her Sally again, and one more time she quieted me down, shattering my last defenses with a smile I hadn't expected to see again in this life. She said something more, but waiting for my response, and seeing lack of it—I thought she finally understood that we were not capable of communicating. The vivid power of her glowing autumn eyes requested my full attention. Only then was I able to hear that she had been repeating one word over and over again.

"Neqeaa." This word pulsed, whispered by the light wind born above the sea. "Neqeaa."

I was at a complete loss. For a moment, I stood numbly listening to the echo of that one word. Again, I couldn't help myself and tried to move closer. Her hand sprung up like a stop sign. I stopped, frustrated, and in desperation, I started to repeat after her, "Neqeaa, neqeaa, neqeaa," thinking that it could be some kind of mantra she used to calm people. I closed my eyes, our voices soaring high over the beach in unison.

Unfortunately I kept them closed for too long, fascinated with the sound of our voices singing together again. Suddenly all I could hear was only my part of the song. Sally…she was gone. There was no sign of her, no movement, not even the slightest rustle of shifting sand could be heard. Perfect peace shielded this part of the Cote d'Azur.

I rushed toward the boat, but when I reached the water, the boat was gone too. Terrified, I started to run back and forth along the shore in my search for Sally, but there was no sign of her presence.

My fruitless quest to find her guided me back to the crowded area of the beach. I saw groups of people sitting on the shore, most of them with candles still lit, and I grasped the reality—my search for this mirage was pointless. Sally, was it really you? That was why you wanted me here? If so, where have you gone? What should I do? I knew I wouldn't find her, I wasn't even sure if what I had just seen was real, or if it was mere delusion haunting my worn-out mind. I didn't know what was real anymore.

In a last cry for help, I even approached a couple covered by a heavy colorful quilt. But it was no use—they didn't speak any English. They stared at me, soaked, and sand-pasted, like I was desperately in need of psychiatric help. They were not far off; I started to think of myself as a loony with visions of ghosts. Kicking wet sand into the water, I guarded the shore long into the night, until the first reasonable solution came to me. Jean-Paul—I have to find him right now. I didn't wait for another sunrise spectacle. Leaving puffy clouds of sand behind me, I dashed toward the center of the village.

Chapter 15

I barged through the door of the Hotel Europa, pushing the glass door's heavy metal frame almost off the hinges with one sharp move. At three in the morning, the only light came from the lamp on the reception desk. I bent over the counter, somehow expecting to find Jean-Paul sleeping behind it. No one was hidden there, of course, and I had to laugh at my own stupidity. But just to make sure—my hope inflamed by the memory of tonight's mysterious event by the sea—I launched myself through the dining area, and even the kitchen—Jean-Paul was nowhere to be found. Disappointed, I persuaded myself to go back to my room and wait until dawn. But not before I tried to call Pete one more time.

The phone fell to the floor from my shaking hands several times. Calming myself, I picked it back up. The promising tone coming from the receiver made me dial the Pete's number quickly. He wasn't answering, so I let the phone ring for a while. Why isn't the voice mail picking up? I waited several minutes more, frustrated by the monotony of the rhythmic sound in my ear, but I could only take it for so long. Finally, I tossed the receiver back, and I raced to my small room like a bullet bouncing from wall to wall. I couldn't pacify myself so, after half an hour, I went back downstairs to see if anyone was there. If there were, it would have been a lonely ghost partying in the emptiness of the first floor.

Several attempts to reach Pete netted the same negative results. In those unsuccessful visits I made downstairs, my head ultimately refused to cooperate. I had to get some rest. But I couldn't; it wasn't possible. Even a steamy shower didn't ease my ache. Crumpled on the bed, all I could think about was Sally. Like the replay of the same fragment of a movie, over and over again, I saw her raised hand stopping me just a split second before I could touch her. Her persuasive words echoed inside my brain. "Neqeaa." Half in the edgy doze—half in self-inflicted lethargy, I intoxicated myself with the fading memories of a time long gone, entwined with indistinct paintings from tonight.

I jumped out of bed as the first stirrings of life echoed from the main floor. It was just past five. Not too much sleep for tonight, but it has to do. My hopes rose of seeing Jean-Paul, as I darted downstairs, taking long thumping jumps over several steps at a time. Someone stood in the kitchen's swinging door.

"Jean-Paul," I shouted.

First I saw paper grocery bags splashing on the floor, and then the dull sound of their contents rolling over behind the bar. I was scared, and it wasn't a joke. The person I faced seemed to me more annoyed than surprised. Afraid for my own well-being, I stopped right in front of someone I assumed was either a cook, or more likely, a cook's helper. She was as tall as me, but I wouldn't go the distance with her. One wrong move and I would have to learn how to call an ambulance in French.

"Merde!" she said, assessing the damage with one quick look. Her voice sounded warmer than I expected under the circumstances, but I kept my guard up, just in case.

"Bonjour," I said, using my sweetest voice.

She appraised me closely for a moment. Then unexpectedly she grinned, exhibiting long strong teeth, perhaps satisfied that my condition was not due to drugs or alcohol.

"Bonjour, Monsieur." She had to make an effort to bend down as she started to gather the scattered groceries. In an instant, I dove under the bar, guided by the smell of freshly baked rolls. I skipped the shattered eggs nearby, leaving them as they were. I didn't think they would be of use anymore.

"Good morning," I said, with the fragile optimism that she would speak English. "How are you this morning?" As soon as I said that, I regretted it.

"Est-ce que vous voyez ce que avez-vous fait? Que faites-vous ici si tôt? Comment puis-je vous aider, Monsieur?" she said, slowly hoisting herself up. The stumped expression in her eyes convinced me she didn't understand what I was saying, so I decided to give it a shot in my recently acquired and very limited French.

"Je vudrais...Jean-Paul," I said.

"Je ne comprends pas de quoi parlez-vous?" she said slowly.

"Je vudrais…parler…" This time I used visual prompts to illustrate his arrival. "Jean-Paul."

"Oh, oui, oui." She nodded. "Jean-Paul."

"Jean-Paul? Oui, oui," I said, involuntarily mimicking her.

"Jean-Paul?" she repeated.

"Yes, Jean-Paul." I was happy with the effect of my multi-lingual abilities.

"À cette heure? Vous avez peru la tête! Il est très tôt. Comment dois-je le savoir?" She frowned. "Jean-Paul viendra peut-être seulement dans deux heures." She turned around as if she was trying to find some kind of help. She placed what remained of her groceries on the bar's counter, and walked out to the reception area. I was right behind her. Approaching the desk, she pointed to the old clock ticking slowly on the wall.

"Il sera ici dans deux heures, après sept heures."

"What?" I whispered.

She waved her hand in the air and said "Sept," extending the open palm of one hand, and two fingers of the other in front of my eyes. "Jean-Paul. Sept."

"Oh, thank you…well, merci," I said, and pushed the warm rolls I held in her direction. She secured them in her iron clutch. I turned around, and I was walking up the stairs when the sound of her loud complaints reached my ears. The most common word I perceived was "merde."

Another long and steamy shower impaired my hearing, at least until I turned on the coffee maker on the credenza. With the aroma of the dense umber brew influencing all of my taste receptors, I waited on the bed, savoring the heavenly cocktail that would have been the envy of any big name coffee chain back home. They served mere coffee-flavored water—the pseudo coffee—compared to the rich nectar I had brewed myself in a matter of minutes.

Just before seven, I walked back downstairs yet again. I took one of the chairs by the wall, and sat on its edge. It was quite homely down here—quaint and old-fashioned. No major renovation had been done within, maybe the last thirty years; nevertheless, it seemed congenial and inviting. A surprisingly tuneful woman's voice sang a French ballad, complementing the male one coming from the radio. I tried not to make any assumption about the singing female; I wanted to keep that comfy feeling for a while.

But my serenity didn't last long. A gentle nudge jolted me back to reality. I raised my head—Jean-Paul stood in front of me, again showing off his perfect smile.

"Good morning, Monsieur Clatt. Why are you sleeping here? Is there something wrong with the room? Or, maybe, did you go out last night and came back too late, huh, Monsieur Clatt?" He smiled, but his eyes were carefully observing me.

"The room is fine, thanks." I was glad I could catch his subtle attempts to test me. I didn't know where that was leading me, but at least I was aware of it. "I did go out last night, but it wasn't what you are thinking," I added.

"Wasn't it one grand celebration?" Jean-Paul said.

"It was unforgettable. I've never seen such a procession in my life," I answered honestly.

"So how was the party?" Jean-Paul added quickly.

"A party?"

"You know, Monsieur Clatt, there is always a party lasting until the next morning, even longer."

"Actually, I didn't go to any party." I thought I said it too fast.

"No party, huh?" His lips formed a sad quarter of the moon shape. "Such a fine young man and no party? It's hard for me to imagine."

"Jean-Paul, can we talk?" I asked, and tipped my head toward one of the empty tables in the dining area.

"Of course, Monsieur Clatt, let's talk," said Jean-Paul as we relocated to the table. "I'm always ready to talk with my dearest guest." He smiled. "But first, let me take care of the business. I'll be back in a few minutes. I will have the cook get you some coffee. Yes, let's drink some coffee, that's what we need," he reassured himself, and ran toward the kitchen door. "Would you like some croissants?" he shouted, but I couldn't answer in time before he disappeared. I slowly took a place at the same table as yesterday.

The cook never materialized, but if the woman I met a couple of hours ago was a cook, I could identify with her reasoning. After a little while, Jean-Paul was back carrying two coffee cups in one hand, and a large plate with croissants in the other, with the grace of the most competent waiter. He placed one cup in front of me. The overpowering colorful scent I had tasted not too long ago tickled that irresistible tempting sensation again. Even though I remained a little jittery from the coffee I'd had in my room, I claimed the tiny porcelain cup right away.

"Well, Monsieur Clatt, your coffee has been served." He watched me, and then laughed. "Oh, the cook." He paused. "She is too busy. She is late with breakfast, with everything, she said. She always terrorize us, but today…" He whistled and rolled his eyes.

I didn't say anything, just listened as he continued. "She is, how to say it…elle est un peu énervée…a little mad. She told me that someone startled her early morning and she dropped everything. The eggs broken, the milk…She had to go to the store again."

"I am afraid it's my fault," I finally admitted. "I didn't mean to scare her, I just…"

"I know, I know, Monsieur Clatt," he said, still laughing. "She told me everything. Not to worry, she is just that way. Maybe she is rough sometimes, or better most of the time, but she is not a bad person. She is a good cook, and she loves her work. But that's enough of her—tell me what brings you up so early in the morning?"

"Well," I started, and then paused. I didn't know exactly how to begin—how to relate my story so I wouldn't be perceived half as idiotic as I thought I was. The minutes ticked by slowly and I sensed Jean-Paul's eyes trying to read through me. He didn't speak, but waited for me to start. The words tumbled out. In a chaotic, unstable manner, I told him about everything I had experienced last night. It took me a while to realize my flow of short, out-of-syntax sentences hadn't been interrupted with a single question.

"Monsieur Clatt." There was a slight change in his voice. It became even more shadowy than before. "Thank you for confiding in me, but I must say, I am not the right person to explain all of this. I am just an innkeeper. But I think I can help you contact someone who knows a lot more—"

"Does this happen very often?" I asked, wondering if I was the only one so messed up.

Jean-Paul looked up at me. "No, not really," he said. His coffee cup was full, untouched. "The last time I heard about something like that was a long, long time ago."

"When? How long ago?" I asked. So, it isn't only me! That thought gave me some courage.

"Thirty-five years ago, give or take a couple? Something like that…It is history."

"What happened then? Tell me!" I grasped at anything that might enlighten me.

"It was a really long time ago, when your—" Jean-Paul abruptly paused. "I don't remember much." He added, but by the uneven tone of his voice—higher than usual—I recognized it was a yet another half-truth. "Let's not waste our time." His commanding tone was low and misty again. He shot off the chair. "Come with me, Monsieur Clatt; let's see if he is still there."

"Who?" I asked, but Jean-Paul was already halfway to the door. I had no choice but to hurry up and follow him.

Cozy, stone-paved streets lay still in the exhausted aftermath of last night's festivity. People we met on our way seemed to have had as much sleep as I'd had. But at least, they didn't appear to be so miserably lost. I could see their tired faces, and when they noticed us, they smiled and waved as we passed them by.

I had some trouble keeping up with Jean-Paul's pace. By my calculations, he was leading us away from the sea. If we were headed toward the shore, we would have hit it by then, or at least heard the beat of the waves. But all I could hear was the sea gulls' musical wake-up call. I fell a few steps behind him; I hadn't expected such speed from the old man. Just to catch up with him, I would have to run. I was sure I wouldn't be able to get anything out of him right then, and I wasn't in the mood to talk either. "It was a really long time ago, when your—" When my—who? What? What happened thirty-five years ago?

I knew I'd started to scratch the surface of something, and I had a feeling that I was supposed to have at least a vague knowledge of what. But I didn't. Unfortunately for me, I wasn't able to make the connection, so keeping my myriad questions jostling in my head with every step, I kept up with Jean-Paul as best I could.

The rows of tight-knit medieval buildings on both sides of the street abruptly stopped as though cut off by a sharp knife. The village had ended and as far as I could see, there was nothing on the horizon except tall golden-green grass and shrubs leading the way out of the village. Beyond them, groves of trees were reborn in yet another consistent life cycle, covering the feet of the mountains far away.

I made an effort to approach Jean-Paul, but he took a turn onto a hidden path behind dense entwined bushes, a passage that revealed itself only to those who knew where to look. I didn't see it, and would certainly miss it if I had to search for it by myself. I forced my way through the stinging twigs right behind Jean-Paul. Snake-shaped weeds overgrew the cream step stones a short distance beyond the natural gateway. Untouched for ages, their dry, cracking sounds reflected the rhythm of our steps. The trail ended with a clearing large enough to host a little rectangular hut. Its whitewashed walls and thatched roof screamed for remodeling, if not demolition.

Jean-Paul didn't falter, and went straight for the crooked door, with slits big enough to put a hand through. He didn't bother knocking; the hinges gave a long rusty squeal. I stopped just before the threshold opening. After contemplating the risk for a moment, I eventually went in after him, keeping next to the bearing wall, just in case the roof gave way.

Once my eyes adapted to the murky light, the claustrophobic room unveiled a shielded by dove-color hair, dried out, almost mummified man—a skeleton man, I named him—sitting behind a small table. Jean-Paul stood next to him, whispering in his ear. The skeleton man sharply pointed at me a few times, but otherwise listened with his eyes closed. The shock of silence, broken only by Jean-Paul's monotonous murmurings, blended together with the mysterious dimness around me, to create a dreamlike quality. It has been so unreal; I had to poke myself, just to make sure I was there.

Finally, Jean-Paul spoke in English. "Monsieur Clatt, sit down please." The cracked wooden chair grated on the porous lumber of the neglected wooden floor. I hesitated; the half-doubting, half-laughing glare of the skeleton man was unnerving, but I obeyed and found myself sitting directly across from him.

"Monsieur… it is Clatt, isn't it?" If I expected some kind of a rasping sound matching his posture, the skeleton man's smooth voice caught me unguarded.

"Yes, it is," I said automatically.

He speaks English! I must've looked shocked.

"Surprised?" asked the skeleton man.

"I can't say I'm not."

"You should get used to it. One has to learn the language of one's enemy."

"Enemy?"

"Oh, it is a long story—" He laughed, and glanced at Jean-Paul.

"Pierre is the oldest man in the village. The oldest and the wisest, I would say," said Jean-Paul.

"Don't flatter me, boy," said Pierre.

"Most people have forgotten about him already." Jean-Paul didn't react. "But there are some, not too many, unfortunately, who now seek his advice. How do I say it? Il a le plus des connaissances—he possess the best knowledge. He was, well…he still is, a Gardian. He is how would you say it, Il est à la retraite—retired."

"What has all of this got to do with me?" I directed my question to Jean-Paul but my eyes zoomed in on the skeleton man.

"Isn't it you who wanted to know what was happening?" he asked.

"Well—" I said.

"You wanted answers," said Jean-Paul. "Pierre is the only one I know who might help you. So go ahead, the old chap gets tired quicker than he used to." Jean-Paul's loud laugh shook the fragile home. The skeleton man grinned but remained otherwise static, scrutinizing me from under half-closed thin eyelids.

"So, Monsieur Clatt," said Pierre. "Can you tell me what exactly happened last night?"

"Where should I start?" I panicked. "So many things have happened. Do you—"

"Merde! Just tell me, what did she say?" The skeleton man wasn't a patient listener. "This comédien…this young fool here," he pointed at the smiling Jean-Paul, "…already told me the story. What exactly did she say?"

"I remember only one word—" I thought I saw their eyes meet for a split second.

"Well, what was it, then?" shouted Pierre.

"Neqeaa?" I whispered.

"Neqeaa?" he repeated. "Nothing else?"

"I didn't understand anything else. Only this one word. She kept repeating it over and over. She even made me repeat it with her."

The skeleton man closed his eyes, and leaned over his decaying desk. Jean-Paul was silent too. He seemed to fall into the same deep meditation the skeleton man was in. I sat quietly for a while, but then I couldn't wait any longer. I called up all the courage I had in me and asked, "Can either of you tell me what is going on?"

No answer.

"Who was that woman?" I tried again. Again all I got was silence. I stood up and shouted, "Come on, can somebody tell me who she was? Why did she look like my wife? What the hell is going on here?"

No words came from either of them. They hadn't moved an inch, neither the skeleton man at his desk, nor Jean-Paul, tightly gripping the man's chair. I sat back, exhausted with frustration.

"Please," I dropped to my knees. "Please tell me before I really go nuts."

"Stand up, you fool; it's not me you should be kneeling to." Pierre's voice boldly cut the long curtain of muteness. "Neqeaa means a cave in Aramaic."

"Aramaic? A cave?" I said. "What this is about?"

"If you want to find out, you have to do it by yourself." He quickly stopped a tirade of my questions I had on my mind. "You have to make a trip."

"A what?" I said. "What kind of trip? I'm on a trip already." I paused, and then added, "Why?"

"A trip, I said," Pierre nearly shouted.

"But—"

"There is no 'but,' Monsieur Clatt," said Jean-Paul.

"Do you want to find out or not?" Pierre's harsh tone was the answer by itself.

Of course I wanted to. After an astonishing acquaintance with the boat and its occupants, who wouldn't want to find out what that was all about? "Yes, I do. But—" I saw the impatience growing in the skeleton man's eyes. "I'm going back home in…" I tried to count how many days, but I couldn't. "The day after tomorrow, this Saturday. I'm not sure I have enough time for any trips."

"Did I say how long it would take?" he said. "I only said you have to take a trip if you want to find out the truth. If you want the truth—you have to find it out by yourself. No one is able to help you, no one."

I should've memorized this term already. "I know," I said.

"So listen carefully, you jeune home, and don't make an old man nervous. You don't have the slightest idea how much time you need or have. Let's just say you have enough of it."

"OK, OK," I said slowly. I could swear that Jean-Paul was trying to hide a smile, but when I turned to him, he was as serious as I'd ever seen him.

"Then—" the old man turned around and, after a short search on the floor behind him, produced a road map. He unfolded it impatiently, and placed it on the table. "Here is where you will go." He pointed to the red sign already drawn with permanent marker on a vast green area on the map.

"Where?" I asked.

"Right there, don't you see it? It's me who is almost blind," Pierre said and pointed again. "And you go there by yourself—not with him, not with a guide, not with anybody. Just you. You understand?"

I looked up toward Jean-Paul, but there was no reaction.

"I do," I said. "I think I do."

"Don't think," he said. "Act. Do you know what I mean?"

"Yes," I said, not hesitating a second.

"Good." Pierre stared at me. "Then what are you waiting for?"

"But, wait." I felt stunned. "Why? When? What is out there?" I started to blurt out questions, but one glance was enough for me to take in that this was all I could expect to learn from him. He wouldn't tell me anything more, and even if he decided to speak again, it would only be the phrase I had already memorized: "You have to find out by yourself." And what am I supposed to do? What did Sally have to do with Saint Sara, and a woman on the beach, who looked like Sally? It was Sally herself—wasn't it? And why did she use this strange language? Aramaic—never heard of such. She asked me to go to a cave. A cave? Who was she?

Chapter 16

I saw the familiar, faded letters on the canopy above the door as we turned onto the side street in the center of Saintes-Maries-de-la-Mer. No exchange of thoughts, not even a single word interrupted our long walk from the skeleton man's hideout. Puzzled by this latest experience, I started to believe it would be much better not to think ahead too far, much safer for me, at least, to just accept everything as it was progressing. Miniature signs started gradually to point in the direction where all of this was heading, but I didn't think I wasn't ready for it, not yet. We were about to go inside, when I stopped. I didn't recognize it at first, but as it happened to be just a few feet from me, its presence here at the Hotel Europa shook me.

"What is that thing doing here?" I pointed to the burgundy Renault parked right in front of the hotel's entrance.

"What, Monsieur Clatt?" asked Jean-Paul. "Oh, Une voiture…your rental car. I forgot to tell you. I'm sorry."

"But how did you — ?" For a moment I think I had left the key in the room, but when I patted my pockets, I felt the hard outline of the car key. "How did you get it over here without the key?"

"Monsieur Clatt, let me tell you this, if I may," said Jean-Paul. "You don't always need a key to open a door. All that you need is a will."

"I'm afraid I don't get it," I said.

"Not to worry, Monsieur Clatt. Everything is fine. You can leave in no time," said Jean-Paul. Then he added, "Oh, there is a lunch for you, you didn't eat anything except croissant. It's ham and cheese baguette—you'll see, you'll like it."

"I'm sure I will," I said, thinking, is there anything else to surprise me today?

"Here it is," said Jean-Paul, handing me a folded map. "Monsieur Clatt, please make sure you follow directions; everything is marked for you."

"What if I get lost?"

"Monsieur Clatt, you won't. I am sure you won't." Jean-Paul opened the driver's door before I took out the key.

"Maybe I should get my—"

"Just go, Monsieur Clatt, do not waste time, please. Everything will be fine. Trust me."

Trust. I don't have much of a supply anymore. It's been drained out by the gallons.

"It's time, Monsieur Clatt," he added. "You should leave, now."

I left just as I was. There was no time to get up to my room to pack, to change—not even three whole days left to my departure, and now I'd gotten myself into an unexpected expedition to…That was one of my questions: to where? Even though I hadn't slept much for the last few nights, I didn't feel tired. To my astonishment, I perceived myself as fresh and ready, like I was ten years younger. I attributed it to the wonderful Mediterranean climate, and a French baguette washed down with some water from the bottle I found inside my car as well.

The road, which seemed friendly at the beginning of my trip, became narrower as it whipped and turned with the elevation. Then on the other side of the hill, it straightened itself out, shooting ahead through a vast plain of tall waving grass. Far away in the distance stood the towering solid barrier of a brown cliff guarded by a thick cover of oaks, bursting with new green shoots. It bullied its way through the greenery, soaring over the nearly perfect level plane. The sun leaned gradually toward the west when I left behind the last informational sign leading to Sainte Baume.

After a short drive up the massif, I consulted Pierre's map and pulled into the parking lot of the Hotellierie of La Sainte Baume, which he had marked as a stopping point for me. Immediately I jumped out of the car and stretched. Mist hung over the cool mountain air, colored with the scent of wild thyme. Tourists had gathered around, trying to measure their height against the enormous cliff as it proudly presented its magnificence to the crowd.

Carved into the cliff's limestone face was a structure, its walls barely visible above the tree line. I stood with the tourists for a while, and then, right after passing the remnant of the oak tree, shaped into the form of a woman who welcomed me, I had to decide to take one of the two routes leading to the grotto. I took the worn trail winding through the forest. Pieces of rock formed large stepping-stones, which led me up the hill. Signs requesting silence rose occasionally from the mossy ground of the woods, my only companions on my climb up the massif's slope.

According to the brief description located on the back side of Pierre's map, the enormous cave incised by nature into the thick face of the cliff was Mary Magdalene's place of solitude for her final thirty years. I didn't know that fact, even more, I didn't know much about what had happened after the death of Jesus, anyway. So, as I was surprised by another legend, any connections to Sally seemed very vague, if nonexistent. But if that was what Sally, or the Sally from the beach last night wanted, I went with the flow, as in the saying. If this was where she has led me, well then here I was.

The cave's entrance, enclosed now with a brick wall and an encompassing wrought-iron fence, gave an impression more severe than one would expect. To my surprise, the heavy wooden door opened easily. Little daylight filtered through the stained glass windows installed above, between the wall and the natural ceiling of the cave. If not for the flames of numerous candles, shadows would cover the enormous cavern.

To the side of the grotto stood a monumental white chapel with an altar, under which the relics were put to rest. Next to the chapel there were stairs leading to the larger-than-life sculpture of what I thought was the saint. For a moment, I thought I heard the muted sound of dripping, like the flow of pure water from a hidden spring. In awe, I observed the fascinating architecture as I seated myself on the last of the hand-hewn wooden-plank pews, grouped on both sides of the chapel, oblivious to people around me.

What has this got to do with me? That question had been in my head for so long, I accepted the fact I might as well have been born with it.

I fervently anticipated something—anything—to happen. Judging from the events of the last three days, it would be natural to predict an unusual ending to this evening. What is the real reason Sally wanted me here? Did she insist last night on the beach, or was it only my imagination? Why all the mystery? Maybe I mispronounced the only word she was repeating? No, I haven't, I couldn't. I felt I should know the answers to some of these questions, but I was sure I'd missed something along the way. My problem was I had no idea what I had failed to notice. What does she want?

As though paralyzed, I didn't move for maybe an hour. Then, wearied by the constant anticipation, I started to count the number of people who came into the grotto. Soon I changed the subject of my attention to the people who were looking around as they entered, and a while later, I switched to those who walked directly to the altar. Still, there was nothing to guide me, to provide the answers to my questions.

Disenchanted, I gave up hope, and prepared to leave, but at the last moment, I changed my decision. I would take a quick break outside the cave, and then come back and wait a little longer. But not more than another hour, I promised myself. Well, I'm going to give it a try until they close the cave. I made the correction. I hope I will be able to find my way back then.

As I stood, stretching my legs, a large group of visitors entered the grotto and nearly filled the benches, forming live layers around me. The only way to leave this thick hedge of bodies was to force my way through to the back along the wall of the grotto. A slender path wound along between the wall and my bench, leading behind other occupied pews. The opening seemed wide enough to let me pass by without disturbing anyone.

I started carefully meandering toward the exit. Gradually, with patience I never expected I had, I drew close to the clearing, when my shoes lost traction on the slippery stone floor. My feet flew out from under me and my head and shoulders violently met the wall.

Expecting to hear snickers—or at least muffled chuckles—from nearby witnesses, I turned around to apologize. At once, the physical pain was gone. I completely forgot about my hurting face and bruised hands. The anesthesia of horror took full effect. All I saw was witless obscurity around me, pierced only by a wide stream of weakening light. There was no altar, no candles, no benches, not even a sculpture—just the measureless, oppressive emptiness. The quietness of the dim cave played eccentric notes inside my head, and curled inside the cold arms of the recess in the wall. I expected the worst.

This doesn't make any sense! I don't want answers anymore. It's cold. I've had enough of this, I want out!

After a while, I realized nothing had stopped me when I moved my foot, nothing had jumped on me, nor I was chained to the wall like I felt I was. At least that was an improvement. Using the wall as a support I started to slide along in the direction of the faint light, hoping it came from one of the stained glass windows. The angular and abrasive surface was doing everything in its power to stop me. But, sacrificing my back, I pushed forward at an agonizing pace. The exit was so close; right behind the next bow of the scoured limestone—a few more steps and I would be free from the cold mountain.

Then, seeing the plain, unobstructed opening of the cave mouth made me stop in agony. The gate and wall were missing. I peered out—there was nothing except the last call of the sun for the day. Everything else—everything that used to be human-made, everything I had seen on my arrival here—was gone. It seemed like it was never here, as if I had imagined the wall, the stained-glass windows, the wooden gate, and the fence. None of it had ever existed. Only the aroma of wild thyme floating from the forest below reminded me exactly where I was.

Unsure of myself, I let go of the wall, tripping on the rugged floor, and ran out through the natural entrance of the cave. I stopped just by the steep decline of the massif. I couldn't decide if I should stay there and wait for help in the morning, or risk the late evening walk through the barely-visible pass leading down.

No, I'm just hallucinating. It's a concussion. Everything will be fine. Relax. I closed my eyes. Once I open them, everything will be normal. On three…One…two…and…everything remained unchanged. No signs of civilization whatsoever. I stood on the verge of the sheer chasm in the middle of nowhere, staring at the virgin piece of land. I have lost it. I was convinced by then. How do I ever get out of this? I hope they have a pill that can help me. I have to see a doctor when I get back. If…

I took a few steps toward the edge of the hill and peeked down over the rim. But it only confirmed my worst fears—nothing down there either. Then I decided, the option of staying here alone didn't appeal to me at all. I turned around, ready to work my way down the hill. I didn't even take a first step when my knees nearly buckled. I underwent a short-lived urge to run away, yet I couldn't move. In the dim evening light, in the entrance to the cave, a woman stood in exactly the same spot where I had only minutes before. The cloak and the veil over her hair perfectly harmonized with the face of the rocks. I knew it! I knew it! Suddenly I wasn't fearful. As I drew closer, her cherry hair slipped out of the veil, and her slim hand reached to pull it back in.

Is it for real? Again, I questioned my sanity. But the vision was so vivid and true it just about made my heart crush my rib cage. My remaining logic demanded the impossibility of what I was seeing. Sally was dead—it must be a mirage, again. Sally observed my struggle; it seemed she was holding something in her hands while standing nearby.

Logically, it couldn't be; nonetheless, I believed it was. I felt it in every cell of my battered body. I couldn't stand it any longer, and rushed toward her, mindless of the pain, the slippery terrace, anything. I was only a few feet away when she hid whatever she was holding beneath her cloak, and extended her hand wordlessly. Again? Why is she doing that? With that minimal gesture, she made me stop instantly. Not that I wanted to, but she requested it, and I obeyed her wish. Exhausted, resigned, and mystified, I watched her from the distance she had chosen to leave between us.

"Sally," I shouted, but there was no answer. "Sally," I said again. "Honey, it's me."

She spoke out tenderly; her voice flew over the cliff and echoed in my brain with unfamiliar phrases. Listening to her soft tone contrasting with the resonating nasal quality, I was sure she was speaking in the same language I had heard moments ago, by the boat, but it didn't help at all. She was not repeating herself as she had the last time. At least, I wasn't able to distinguish any similar pattern. I knew it was no use anyway—there was no one here to translate. It was just the two of us on a deserted mountain.

She kept talking, ignoring the drape of the night closing around us. From time to time, she drew shapes in the air with her hands, like a child's rudimentary pictures. The only problem was that, even with her cryptic sign language, I couldn't figure out anything she was trying to express. I was overwhelmed. I couldn't comprehend anything at that moment, however straightforward. Only when she lifted her voice a notch, and sharply pointed behind me, did I awaken from my sweet lassitude.

My eyes followed her hand and I guessed she was telling me about the dusk descending over the quiet landscape. She smiled when I finally reacted, and her smile ignited all my memories. The way she smiled, with her lips twitching vaguely, her eyelids half open, she seemed so vulnerable, so undecided and exposed, just like she always had. The picture of her was so deeply ingrained in me—it was so missed, so dreamed of, so unexpected and improbable, that I lost the last of my defensive instincts.

Her hands fluttered. Is she inviting me in? I thought. I felt a flicker of brief uneasiness. Then I didn't waver at all. She was my wife; I didn't know how it was possible, but she was. I was certain that whatever was going on, and whoever had arranged this strange journey, hadn't done it to hurt me. She wouldn't let that happen. Deep inside, I was sure of it. I trusted her. It was beyond trust; I felt an unabridged devotion unshaken even by the distance she demanded when, once more, I tried to approach her. Again, her smooth hand rose immediately with a strength of will, which could not be denied.

Why won't you let me touch you? Again, I stopped—this time close enough to observe her face. In the waning light, her sallow olive skin was covered with more wrinkles than I remembered. I hadn't noticed that before, but standing not more than three feet from her, they were impossible to miss.

Taking the wild thyme bouquet with us instead of candles, we entered the vast grotto, which seemed small and cozy when filled with the gloom of the cool night. She graciously strolled across the uneven floor, keeping the distance between us within her personal comfort level, and I held myself together, not making any sudden moves. After a while, I could barely see her. Like a bat, using abilities I never dreamed I possessed, I was aware of—rather than saw—her in front of me.

A little enclosure sculpted in the naked rock revealed itself in one of the walls. She motioned toward a large stone, indicating I should lie down. For the first time, I didn't need any more explanation. This would be the most uncomfortable bed I'd slept in ever, but in spite of everything, it was closer to my wife than I ever thought would be possible. I nodded my head in agreement. She smiled but before I could say a word, she vanished into the dim heart of the grotto.

I never thought that the cold coarse surface of a rock could be so warm and comforting, but it didn't help—I wouldn't sleep anyway. I drank some water from the harsh clay bowl I blindly discovered by my stone bed. It was pure and cold, most likely born right here, down in the cave's bottom. I didn't feel hungry, the baguette I had earlier was more than enough for me. Mystified and clueless, my eyes searched the darkness concealing the rough ceiling of the cave high above me. I tried to understand, but it was beyond my reach, beyond my comprehension, out of my range. I was dependent on my own beliefs, unverifiable but true.

I had the notion that something or someone had prearranged and controlled whatever was happening to me. I was a mere pawn, playing out its assigned role. It seemed that I wasn't even offered any options; it seemed like my destiny. The strangest part was that I didn't mind. I did not intend to run away. I wanted to stay right here. Weirdly enough, I felt safer here than back at home. It was an eccentric impression, considering the fact I had no idea where I was, and how, or why, Sally was here.

Is it Sally? It must be! I was confident it was she. No one else could ever calm my heart, or dispel my fears. Only Sally could cast such a spell over me. I wanted to stay with her for as long as I could, even if I never touched her again. It was irrelevant. What mattered the most, was that she was here with me again. Even in this clammy cave, I could breathe her presence. But—

Rosie! My thoughts flew home, but came back peaceful and soothed. I convinced myself that Pete was there for Rosie. I was sure he would do everything in his power to take good care of her. The unusual circumstances of not being able to reach him for the last couple of days no longer caused anxiety. It didn't matter. Nothing mattered where I was at that moment.

I must have dozed off, because the next thing I recognized was the first arrow of sunlight gently probing inside the grotto. Vigilantly, little by little, it moved toward the middle of the cave, then illuminated the cathedral interior and chased away the shadows of the night.

I stretched and walked outside, inhaling the fragrant morning mist. Sally was already outside, waiting for me, sitting on the large round limestone boulder with her face lit by the sunlight. She smiled. As I approached her, I wondered what words I should use to greet her, but nothing came out except common "Good morning." She didn't answer, her eyes riveted on me. Again, I thought I saw a movement of her hands concealing something under her cloak. I felt her eyes penetrating me, searching inside. I didn't want to see her upraised hand again, so I kept my distance. The climbing sun, uncensored by clouds, caused me to shade my eyes to see her better.

The glow of the morning reflected against the weathered wall of the mountain behind her. She was wearing the same red cloak over her green tunic, threadbare in the daylight. The light veil wasn't strong enough to fully hide her wine-colored hair, which streamed with long ashen streaks around her wrinkled neck.

"What is going on?" I said aloud, and immediately realized that I wasn't going to receive an answer.

"Aaqrebo deam aenaa." Sally said. And before she started to walk she made a gesture toward a leather satchel and water skin waiting next to the stone.

"I don't know what you are saying," I said.

"Aaqrebo deam aenaa." She turned around and spoke with a smile. The smile I remembered.

I picked up a bag, and a cold water skin, and watched Sally taking small steps, the tiny fragile steps I knew from the bottom of my heart. And then, guided by her shadow, I instinctively followed her downhill.

Chapter 17

Submitting to her swift pace, I walked right behind Sally, bathed in my own sweat. The dry, cool morning air did not keep the sun from frying us up on the open pan of the valley below. Sally didn't appear to be affected, but I could imagine her cloak acting as a good steamer, or perhaps an oven; I was damp under my jeans, and polo. She could at least take off the veil. Keeping a constant tempo, neither stopping nor turning, she marched all morning. It seemed like an eternity to me, until the unscathed, undefiled forest embraced us in its cooling shadows. Silently, we strode down the deserted rock-strewn slope.

Finally, Sally commanded a break. She sat down on the mossy trunk of a fallen tree, and with delicate, aristocratic grace, her hands pulled the cloth off her head, letting the flow of air swirl through her hair. Then she motioned for me to sit next to her. I hesitated for a moment, and then took a seat not more than few feet away.

The touch of wild thyme dissolved in the dewy atmosphere of the woods, soaking into our pores and satisfying us with healing energy. I unplugged the water skin, and tried to hand it over to Sally, but she refused, raising her hand in a familiar motion. It wasn't much different when I opened the satchel, and found a large piece of unleavened bread. But with her eyes she invited me to try. I bit into the heavy, sour-tasting dough flushing it down with the cool mountain water. My fears, if there still were any, were long gone by then. Nothing but peaceful calm filled my heart. Even if I was not able to communicate with her, I felt like she had accepted me, her silent outline resting close to me. I was sure she knew exactly who I was, and my reason for being here with her. She knew she was the reason.

As I observed her from under my half-closed eyelids, I unwillingly gasped. The tiny spider web of wrinkles had transformed into a deep cloud of furrows. They began at the corners of her eyes as she stared intently into the woods. Lines crawled along the side of her face and around her ears, to hide themselves beneath her silvered hair.

I traced her fixed look at something in the distance—a wobbly object flashed between the trees. It approached us at a steady pace, but only when it came into view from behind a tree— maybe thirty yards from us—was I able to identify the shape of a walking man. Wearing a sunburned light tunic, I was surprised to see him covered with a thick mantle. Using a heavy coat in this kind of the weather? That's unique. I'm dying from overheating. With the layer of thick material suspended on his wide shoulders, the black-bearded man turned his head back and forth, perhaps in search of something lost. Scanning the carpet of the forest, he drew closer to us, striding with the sure, deliberate steps of a sailor.

He acted as if he wasn't aware of our presence at all, which was hard to imagine, considering his proximity. I turned to Sally, waiting for some kind of reaction, but she remained still, her eyes following the stranger's movements. By then, he was right in front of us—so near I easily could touch him if I extended my arm. He stopped and his head rose slowly, presenting a pair of cold, coal-like eyes that penetrated the air with intensity. Is he afraid or is he unwilling to ask for help? I thought, as I waited for Sally to speak. But the stranger turned away and moved on through the woods at his previous pace. Strange. Has he even seen us? I glanced at Sally, as she closely studied my face. When our eyes met, she only smiled. Rising to her feet, she slid off the tree trunk.

"Aaqrebo," she said, as she picked up the faint path leading through the forest.

After another hour or so, our pace slowed a bit as we descended to the edge of the wide plain spreading out at the bottom of the hill. Golden green oak and beech trees, pink and violet shrubs, and bushes of lavender, rosemary, and thyme, yews, and occasionally a wonder—a lime tree—scattered all the way to a thick green border, which girded the horizon, marked the flat land. The walk became a little more bearable as the pressure in my calves eased. I hadn't hiked in years.

The wrinkles on Sally's face grew deeper every time I glanced her way; her hair painted white. Her tiny, fragile form started to bend toward the ground at a more pronounced angle than I would expect from a woman my age. Shouldn't she be my age? She appeared so last night. Her butterfly steps were gone, replaced by the poorly balanced shuffle of stiff legs, carefully taking one step after another. She is tired. She is awfully tired; it doesn't look good. Whatever it is, whatever is going on, we should stop right now, I thought, and I was eager to say something. She should take a break for a moment, rest awhile, drink some water, eat something; I was sure she was going to collapse. But I said nothing. If she only could understand me! As she slowly hobbled forward, I silently followed her steps, troubled by my muddled thoughts.

The sun had been wrapping up its daily matters as we took another short break in the shadow of a large group of trees. This tiny little forest had grown in the middle of the open plain. I wiped the sweat off my face, and searched for some cool place to rest. I sat with my back against a tree stump for only a moment. The bark of the tree annoyed me, scraping my shoulders with its scratchy teeth. I lay down on the dry, yellow forest fleece.

Across from me, Sally sat up straight with her eyes closed, searching for a whiff of the rustling draft that roved between the trees. She had a natural gift that was granted to not too many people. She attracted attention—not for any apparent reason—just because she was. Her weak hands, exposed by the rolled up sleeves of her cloak, rested on her knees. Dried out by the sun and wind, her tired head leaned against the tree. Yet, every detail had been graceful. In my heart, it was my wife in front of me—even taking into account everything I had witnessed so far. For a reason I couldn't explain, she was different, but she was still my wife. Sally— no one else—and I wanted to hold on to this daydream for as long as I could. Does it really matter where are we going? This question drifted out of out nowhere. I set it aside. I was sure it was irrelevant.

We kept walking farther away from the mountains until we entered the damp, broad woods again. With every step, the forest became thicker, veiling us in its rustling arms as we took a hardly noticeable trail naturally carved around each rock and tree. Sally hadn't dawdled even for a moment. No break this time; Sally held her own steady speed as we strolled through the endless serpentine forest. Only the sounds of rushing gusts bending the branches high in the crowns of the trees, and the crunching underbrush under our feet kept us company, playing a symphony of the day's end.

We had walked quite a distance through the forest glade, and I had begun to think about a rest stop. Suddenly I spotted a man and a woman of indeterminate age sitting on the mossy ground by the trunk of a tree ahead of us. They wore similar dark—almost black—cloaks. I didn't think Sally had noticed them yet—even though we were close enough to hear them breathe. Bent forward, her back arched in a hairpin curve, Sally kept walking, as if passing them by. Then, she abruptly stopped right in front of the couple on the ground. With an effort that showed torture only in her clear eyes, she straightened up. Then she smiled. Her smile was sincere—

not the polite smile anyone can produce at will—but a peaceful beam directed only at these strangers.

But these strangers didn't accept it well. It seemed her serene attitude had awakened feelings long hidden. With a shriek of anger, they both jumped up and shouted in high-pitched, short, spiky phrases. They hurriedly backed several yards away, trying to keep their distance from her. Oblivious to my presence, their aggressive barks became louder and more intense. The woman bent down, grabbed a solid wooden stick, weighed it in her hands for a moment, and then, with a battle cry, she threw it at Sally. The man threw a much thicker stick at her only moments later.

Frozen in place for a split second, I wondered how I could help Sally avoid contact with the flying branches. Then automatically, without any further delay I did what had to be done. Bag and water skin dropped, I ran toward her, prepared to knock her out of the path. Her quivering hands did not rise in self-defense, as they should, but remained at her sides, making her even more vulnerable.

Sally didn't move; she stood where she was, training more attention to the couple who had launched the attack than on the dangerously heavy weapons flying toward her. Splitting the air with the swooshing sound of muffled rotors, both sticks closed in on the defenseless woman. Even if she decided to cover herself, her frail hands were no match for the speeding wood. Her brave face was creased and pale as she waited. I jumped. I was a step or two away from carrying her to safety when everything around us halted for a moment. I wasn't sure who was more astounded—those two strangers or I. Until that moment, they obviously rejoiced to see that their sticks were about to hit the target with unexpected precision. I, on the other hand, charged in to prevent it.

We all watched as the rigid wooden sticks dematerialized. They did not simply fall to the ground—just inches before they hit the Sally's face, they disintegrated right in the front of our eyes. What the—? Even the sultriness of the forest couldn't protect me from the icy chill in my spine. Only moments ago, I had searched for a cooling breeze; now I felt like a runner who just got caught in a frosty blizzard. I observed this spectacle with bulging eyes. I didn't think any mind was capable of understanding exactly what had just happened. I gazed at the couple. Stalled, their mouths agape, their eyes targeting one point in front of them, they stood in silence until the first shock wore off. Then the woman started to shout again, and the man joined in. Between their howls of rage, they both spit in Sally's direction with such force that saliva flew a great distance.

Sally focused on them flee. She seemed eager to approach them again, possibly forgiving their hostility, but the man held the woman's hand and backed away, screaming and spewing loudly until they disappeared into the woods.

I could hear their voices as I moved toward Sally. Her eyes were tired, her face distorted in pain, but she remained calm and full of absolution. Slower than usual, her hand rose up to stop me from comforting her. I had no choice but to obey her command. I halted immediately. Did she try to convince me I was not good enough to have the privilege of touching her again, like I used to. Who was she?

There was something inexplicable in her, some quality I was not able to identify. In Sally's presence, I was subjected to extreme tranquility and the ability to forget about the existence of the outside world. I recalled the feeling of being fully alive, so full of happiness, so full of joy, so filled with promise. All these things remained the same, except they seemed to be a thousand times stronger.

I still couldn't find an answer of what was happening to me. I remembered the first night I arrived in Fox River Valley Gardens. The drunken man in the woods by the fatal road curve saying, "Go there! You must go there." I heard his faint voice. Then Sally's letter with its odd request, Pete, who hid something, the hectic night at the airport, the luggage, Jean-Paul picking me out of the crowd, the

Gypsies, Saint Sara. The boat! Skeleton man speaking perfect English and sending me to…What had happened there in the cave? Sally? She couldn't answer, neither did I; a blank screen rolled over my eyes—just the pure, clear panel of nothing. I wasn't exactly sure where I was, or how I was going to get out of here. But I didn't want to leave, not yet. Not until she made me go. Whatever selective memory brought to me from the past, or whatever future lay ahead of me, my only chance of surviving it was with her help.

Without uttering a word, Sally moved ahead as I followed behind her yet again. But after only after a few steps, she stopped, and straightened her body. I searched the immediate area for possible threats, and spotted someone's head peeking out from behind the trunk of a wide tree. I expected another outburst of screams, but heard only the rustling of leaves and the snap of broken branches, creased by the man's steps, as he slipped from his hiding place. I stood next to her, preparing myself to ward off his attack. He was a big man. Far more than six feet tall, with a thick bull's neck; he had arms that could probably break me in half. As he came close, he centered all his attention on Sally. There was no violence in his large eyes. He dropped to his knees in front of her; a wave of tears fell down his cheeks, his whole body shaken by spasms.

Sally took a step forward and waved her slender hand over his bowed head. Her sign had an instant impact; he calmed down as the ground cover under him soaked up the stream of his tears. His face began to shine in the shadow of the forest with such energy, such illumination; it seemed to radiate all over the area.

He remained motionless as we walked away. After a while, I discreetly looked back. Against the amethyst background of the evening, I could see the indistinct shape of the kneeling man.

The night covered us quickly as our pace slowed down even more. Sally's tunic and cloak seemed to become oversized, hanging on her as if they could slip off at any moment, quivering dangerously with her every step. Through the scant woods ahead, I saw the outline of a building. Is that where are we going?

Surrounded by the forest, other small wooden houses slowly started to take shape out of the dusk. As we approached the edge of the natural defense, their density increased. Covered with a mud plaster with flat roofs, the dwellings were spread around. I couldn't predict if we were walking through the outskirts of some kind of a village, or it was the village itself.

We approached an unpaved road, and Sally turned. She proceeded into the murky shade of a clay path leading away from the buildings. After not more than five minutes we arrived at a little shed, barely visible from the road. Hidden between two wide oaks, its walls miraculously stood upright beneath the dangerously sunken roof.

Sally waved her hand, indicating I should enter. I hesitated. It appeared she wouldn't be going inside with me, and just that thought ate away my courage. She persisted. The twisted door groaned and stopped, half open. I had to squeeze myself by to get inside. Why do you want me to go here?

There was plenty of light outside, compared to the claustrophobic interior. The clammy air inside the empty shed touched me, and after a split second, I ran out. I wanted to ask her what she wanted from me, to somehow get her to tell me what was going on. But Sally was gone in the gloomy, ominous night, leaving me all alone.

I hadn't heard a noise or a word from her before she left. Hoping she had stepped a short distance, I searched around the shed. I even went back to the road and ran back and forth for some time, but I was too afraid to go any farther than a hundred yards or so in both directions of the track. I yelled and howled for help but only the deafness of the night echoed back at me. I was alone for good. I imagined stray ghosts occupied the deadly road, ready to attack me. Hoping I could avoid them, I hid in the seclusion of the shack. I was perfectly aware that it was only an illusion of safety, but for now, it would have to be sufficient.

I finished the bread, but left a few sips of the water in the water skin, hoping it would be enough for tomorrow. And then— then, there wasn't anything else to do. Enfolded by darkness and seated as comfortably as I could get on the hard earthen floor, I wondered why she left me here, but I couldn't come up with a logical explanation. What is logical in this whole situation, anyway? I thought. Sally, who are you? Are you really—? Could it be—? No, it's not possible. I dismissed the thought immediately, afraid of the consequences of such implication. The demanding ordeal through-out the long day, the descent from the grotto, filled with strange, unexplained, nearly mystical occurrences, ending with the fearful search for Sally had depleted all the remaining energy stored in me. Blessed unconsciousness was only seconds away.

Chapter 18

Brilliant and ceaselessly warm waves of the morning started to filter through the slits in the shed's walls, and mud roof, barely supported by the branches woven above my head. If not for the sizable, long cracks, I would probably have missed the sunrise altogether, I had been unable to judge the difference between night, and day while coffined inside. Apparently, overnight I became so used to my dark bedroom, I was on the verge of even liking it. It seemed like I had not spent one night, but weeks in there.

I walked outside. Someone was waiting, sitting on the large craggy limestone not too far from the door. If not for the smile, I wouldn't have recognized her at all. Sally seemed even smaller and feebler than yesterday. Her silver hair was wrapped around the tattered veil, fluttering with every clammy gust. Her shoulders hunched deeply under the weight of time; memories of years passed reflected in the shadows that creased her face. But there was the smile, unmistakable Sally's smile.

"Dmaeabiyn Btsapraa." I heard her voice.

"Good morning," I said, and stretched.

She stood up and pointed toward the group of houses. They were distant, but much closer than I thought last night, the first roof clearly visible.

"Aaqrebo." That was all she said.

But before again leading the way, Sally motioned me to leave the satchel, and water skin by the shed. I obeyed and, with no resistance, I followed her, enslaved by the aura of her presence, staring at every measured step she took on the unpaved, patchy road. It shrank at first, as if in doubt of its purpose, and then transformed itself into a soft and muddy open clay stream leading us inside the village. The first little houses we passed were quiet, the occupants still in a deep sleep. I checked my watch from habit; it worked fine so far, but now it was useless. I must have broken it when I skidded into the wall of the grotto, because it had read nine o'clock whenever I glanced at it since then.

No one else had witnessed our silent march through the ghost village. Undisturbed, we approached a central clearing. In the middle of a courtyard stood a building made of rough, tan stones topped with slate tiles, elevated above the smaller houses with flat clay roofs, arranged more or less evenly on the perimeter. The enormous arched gate, pitted with iron nails, defended its entrance.

I thought the gate was locked until Sally approached it and placed her dry, tired hands on the bare wood. In an instant, she pulled one of the gate's wings with such ease, it could have been built out of cardboard. Then she went inside. Cautiously, I followed her, but I stopped at the threshold. The weighty gate swung closed on me, delivering a stinging punch to my back; I shouldn't have waited so long. The door locked itself in its original position with a noisy sigh. Sally didn't turn back; she passed a long, wide table in the middle of the room, and waited in the shadows at the far end. Sunlight graced the chamber only with its limited presence wading in through the latticed window openings. I joined her, rubbing my sore back. She stood in front of a large, dove-colored marble sarcophagus with subtle horizontal lines of brown intrusions, its lid carefully rested on the floor.

An empty coffin! Is it mine? Wait. The stone—

I couldn't finish my thought as the dispiriting interior of the sarcophagus extended its invitation. A warning in my stomach stopped me from approaching. Standing in front of me until that moment, Sally moved to the side.

"Oaaobelo aekap daleel Dbartaa," she said after a moment, facing me. Using only one hand, she removed her cloak and the veil. Instantly her hair flew out, and fell to her shoulders, then skimmed down, and became invisible in the shadows. A pure white linen tunic wholly covered her frail, tiny body. Her aged face, her petite frame, even more minimized by the darkness, was so delicate, it made me restrain from breathing. But her eyes, clear as diamonds, shone, their pupils fixed upon mine.

"Bkulmedem dkianaa oaksharay," she said, and when I tried to express my inability to comprehend what she said, again all I received was a smile. I heard her tender voice one more time, and then it was gone. I wasn't sure if I blinked, or if a stygian cloud had swathed all the windows in that split second since her last words. The brief concentrated blackness passed so quickly, I wondered if it had actually happened. It lasted only milliseconds, but in that time, its presence felt like infinity. When the sun once more penetrated the windows, Sally was nowhere to be seen. Terrified and desperate, I searched the large room, as if I sought a precious lost jewel. I found myself at the door and pushed it—it was locked. Great! I thought, returning to the sarcophagus. Just what I need. What am I supposed to do? What—?

Crippling shock overpowered the unbridled desire to run. I saw the heavy lid resting tightly on top of the sarcophagus. How did that get there? You would need at least four men to move that thing and—for a moment I was taken aback even more by the outline of a yellowed jar positioned just by the edge of the lid. This really looks familiar. Isn't it the same jar that—?

If I was shocked a second ago, this time a torch had permanently welded me to the floor. Someone knelt beside the sarcophagus. A figure in a gray cloak convulsed with sobs, a piece of cloth drawn over its head. It was too small to be Sally, yet it seemed familiar. A child? The one from the boat? How did this kid get inside this place? Blood roared in my ears. My feet overcame their bonds and I carefully approached the coffin. Like a ghost, I squatted by the corner, my cheek touching its warm surface, and peered at the child. I couldn't explain why, but I was sure it was the same child I'd seen three days ago—the night I first saw Sally on the boat. Its face was not visible, for the child's body leaned against the sarcophagus, clinging to it in a heartbreaking embrace. But there was also something different, something I hadn't detected at first.

"Aemaa." I heard a shy cry.

The voice. Something is not right. The child's voice doesn't fit. Why?

"Aemaa." I heard it again, this time a little louder. "Aemaa."

The constant sob filled the room, deafening my thoughts. I sensed, rather than heard, a noise behind me. The door trembled rhythmically as someone tried to invade the privacy of this moment.

And then it struck me. Not knowing who the child was, I finally untangled the mystery. I understood then the sole reason my wife sent me overseas.

I was filled with an undeniable feeling of confidence in this matter, as if Sally herself had revealed it to me. There was no more uncertainty; everything was as clear as water from the bottom of a cave that I left in the water skin. It was so simple. It was a symbol! Everything led to one clear indication of the future. I was out of breath, my voice absent. When I was finally able to speak again, I could utter only one word.

"Rosie." This child represented her in this otherworldly dimension. I was astonished—it all meant she would be fine. She is fine. Every cell in my body held to that thought.

"Aemaa." The child was still embracing the sarcophagus.

"Aemaa." I heard it again, and the voice melted away into thin air. "Aemaa."

I closed my eyes. Everything that had happened was too bizarre to be possible; the only question was if it was a dream, or if I had had just lost my mind. Or both. I knelt by the sarcophagus and started to pray. It was the first time I could remember that I prayed to God, and I didn't ask for help, only for guidance. I couldn't take it anymore by myself. "Aemaa, Aemaa," rang in my ears, although the child had already silently vanished.

Where am I? I was convinced that, once I had deciphered the message about Rosie, everything would go back to normal. Carefully, with intensified hope, I raised my eyelids. But nothing had changed. I was in the same room, on my knees next to the sarcophagus. Light streamed through the window openings, slicing the shadow just enough to distinguish shapes of the objects inside. Resigned, I stood up and slowly walked toward the gate. I tried, but it didn't open. Well, I'm stuck inside now. So far, so good.

I started to pull and push one wing of the wooden door, using all of the force left in me to break it open, but aside from the loud clatter, it remained locked. Needing some rest to gather myself for yet another round with the stubborn wood, I leaned against it. After a minute or so, I was ready to continue the fight, but I leaped back as I heard the rattle of the turning lock. Someone is coming? How did—?

I hid by the wall, all set to make a run as soon as the door opened. I would run and not look back, I decided.

The door swung open slowly, as if the person behind its wooden panel hesitated. First, a gray-bearded, bald head poked inside, cautiously. He probably heard my pounding. While the head examined the misty space, I backed up a little more, trying to blend with the wall behind me. After a long while, a figure wearing a brown cloak materialized in the doorway. The hefty man who stepped inside was older—perhaps sixty—and was about to close the door, when I bolted from my hideout.

I said the first stupid thing that I could put into words. "Good morning. How are you?" as if passing a stranger on the street.

"Mon Dieu! Il s'est passé exactement comme elle a dit qu'il le ferait," he said, ignoring me as if I wasn't there. I didn't run as I had planned, stunned by his reaction—or rather, by the lack of it. His astounded eyes stared at the far end of the room. Through the opened half of the gate, the sun flooded inside as if it was forbidden before. Now it made up for lost time by lighting up the sarcophagus with its mighty glow. I left him alone, and only when a safe distance from the door, I turned back. But he was already inside. Impulsively, I sprinted back, and pushed against the gate but its brass handle didn't give up.

Something is not right, I thought, looking around. Everything was different than when I walked in here with Sally this morning. I had no idea how long I stood there as my brain adjusted to a most unexpected sight. The buildings made out of mud that I remembered clustered around the large one we entered, were no longer there. I would blame my confusion on my mental exhaustion, if not for one quite plain fact. I now stood on the stone of a paved, open square. No more clay mud road like the one we took through the village. And the houses around the square were built differently. Elevated brick structures with sloping tile roofs rose from the ground bordering the plaza. Yet the atmosphere of the place, its ambiance, remained unaffected. There was more to add to my disbelief.

Two of the most underappreciated inventions of our times were parked on the street. I jogged up to the passenger door of the first one. I had the urge to hug the cars one by one, when a view of a distinguished church, reflected in the car window, caught my attention. I turned. Its massive, partially eroded but at the same time full-of-pride stone walls loomed above me. Its two stained glass windows, like a pair of alert eyes watched everything with un-matched dignity and compassion. I leaned against the warm roof of the car in front of me as my knees threatened to buckle. Puzzled, I listened to the church bells' clamorous invitation. A few people with cameras in their hands passed by heading toward the church gate. I caught myself checking my watch. Six. I checked it again. Is it working? I had to verify it, just to make sure—it was. The second hand circled the dial again. Aemaa. I thought I heard a voice. Aemaa.

I grabbed my pocket; the wallet and car keys were still there. That's perfect, but where am I? Now if I can just get back to the grotto…Determined, I stepped back, my hands scorched from the torrid car. My plane ticket and passport were in my suitcase at Hotel Europa, the car by the cave. I have to get there somehow. No matter how, I just have to get home. Rosie is waiting for me. It happened, as I was afraid it would; Rosie would wake up without me at her side. But I wasn't mad, or even disappointed. The fact was, she came out of the coma only because I decided to follow Sally. I'm sure she will understand.

I stared at the burgundy roof of the car in front of me. My heart lurched, as the car suddenly seemed quite familiar. No way! I walked up to the door, fumbling for the keys. I could already see the map, lying on the seat just where I had left it.

"No way!" I said out loud. "I'll be damned." I tried the key, and it fit perfectly, opening the passenger door. At that moment, I promised myself I'd use discretion when talking about my incidents in France. I wasn't even about to try to find an explanation for how this was possible. I accepted it as a miraculous situation—I had no power or knowledge to explain things, nor was there anything I could change. It was as believable as the existence of UFOs.

My only thoughts now were bound with Rosie.

Once inside, I unfolded the map. What the— I tried not to curse when I noticed that the red cross marking the location of the cave was gone. But a large red circle was drawn around a town called Saint-Maximin-la-Sainte-Baume. I followed the red line, which started in the center of town, and led through the highways to Marseille's airport. I almost forgot—today is the twenty-seventh. My plane. The ticket. My suitcase! I estimated the distance to Saintes-Maries-de-la-Mer, then the time necessary to drive to the airport. The plane is leaving at five. I remembered. I'll make it.

Chapter 19

It was late morning when I arrived back in the small village of Saintes-Maries-de-la-Mer, thankful for Pete's wisdom in renting this Renault for me. As far as I knew, the climate control system installed in European cars was as rare as American cars without one. The extreme heat was so intense, I wouldn't want to think about driving a car, cooled only by the wind blowing through rolled-down windows.

I made my way through the astonishingly sleepy, slim streets, and navigated into the center of the village. The Church of the Three Saints, which held the shrine of Saint Sara in its vast interior, extended an invitation to pay homage to her once again as I passed by. I was tempted to ditch my car, and run to see Sara, to thank her for all her help. Everything started when I met Saint Sara, when I helped to carry her from the waves of the cold sea to touch the unknown land. Unfortunately, I was out of time. Rosie was waiting back home for me; my suitcase containing the ticket and my passport was still in the Hotel Europa, and my flight would leave in the next few hours. You know I am grateful for everything. No words can describe my feelings. I honored Saint Sara again bowing my head.

At first look, the street seemed unchanged. I parked along the tenement houses in the first available space I could find. Currents of spicy, damp air nearly knocked me down as I left the car. I walked slowly, my face tilted down, to minimize the effect of my head being pushed inside a giant dryer. It didn't help much—I craved oxygen. I expected to see the Hotel Europa's fading sign and canopy from a distance. It should be visible along the light curve of the street. When I saw an uneven walkway angling slightly to the right, I stopped, and raised my head. Neither canopy nor sign was in sight. Am I on the wrong street? No! I recalled the blue rectangular street sign at the intersection; it clearly said "Rue Portalet" in white letters. Puffing the heavy air, I jogged toward the place where I remembered Jean-Paul's Hotel Europa must be located.

And it seemed like it was, at least by the shape of it. The white stucco building appeared untouched, but its old-fashioned awning and the sign with the faded "Hotel Europa" logo no longer covered the entrance. But the number, the number 16, was still there just by the door. I glued myself to the glass entrance door. There was no indication of any establishment being there at all. It was barren. Nevertheless, I banged on the door frustrated by the thought that no one would miraculously step out to give my suitcase back.

Well! I stopped, close to cursing. Now what? And before I knew it, I was running back to the intersection to verify the street name again, just to allay my rising doubts. Even if I secretly hoped I had taken the wrong street, when I glanced at the sign it only deepened my fear—it was the right one. What happened to Jean-Paul? Why did he evacuate during the last two or three days? How am I going to find him now? And what about my passport, my ticket? This whole journey made me certain about at least one more thing—I lied, many more times than just once, when I said nothing was going to surprise me anymore.

I confirmed the street's name yet again, and frantically jerked my head around. But the more I searched, the more frustrated I became. It's not possible! This is not happening. I thought about going up to the secluded hut to ask the skeleton-man, Pierre, but my heart sank. Considering all the options, I concluded that my chances of finding him were slim to none.

I reached to open the car door to let the hot air out, when I caught a glimpse of the back seat of my Renault. The sight nearly made me tear the door off its hinges with my bare hands. Why hadn't I checked there before? Tucked into the tight space between the passenger and the rear seat was my black suitcase, partially hidden from view. I tore it out of the car. My plane ticket and passport rested on top of the clothes—I really didn't care about anything else.

All that I could think of right then was Rosie. I couldn't wait to hold her in my arms, to talk with her, and to hear her voice again. I could imagine how she would be terrified by everything that had happened to her, and I hoped Pete would be extremely gentle and cautious when talking about Sally. Maybe he hasn't said anything, yet. It would be better if I told her about that. I'll have to ask him to say nothing until I get back.

I didn't pay any attention to how fast I was traveling until I approached the Marseille airport. I drove like a maniac through the loop circling the airport, missing all the exits to the terminals. Finally, I found myself back on the highway again. At the last second, I spotted another exit sign leading back to the airport and veered sharply to the right amid the cannonade of honking horns and screaming brakes. This time, I tried to be more careful on the loop, observing all the road signs. I spotted the rental car return logo, and followed it. Using the express return feature saved me the time I had lost circling the loop. It was too late when I thought about filling up the tank. It will be a hell of a bill for Pete. It was only five days, but the mileage, and now the gas…Somehow, I will have to pay him back.

I had more than a couple of hours, and decided to check in as soon as possible. Being grateful I wouldn't have to pass near the Luggage Service enclosure I ran the escalator to the second floor. The departure hall was a pleasant relief from the mucky air outside, but the serpentine queues of harshly indifferent people made me uncomfortable. Patience was an unknown term for me—I had the irresistible urge to act. I found a phone hung below a fancy Plexiglas hat and dialed Pete. What is going on over there? I haven't been able to reach you at all, and now the answering machine is picking up? It's twenty past seven in the morning back home. Where are you?

"Pete, Joe here. Finally! I got through to you. I'm flying back today, but don't worry—you don't have to pick me up. I'll tell you everything when I see you. The hospital, let's meet there. I'll go there right after I land tonight. And please, please if you haven't yet, please don't tell Rosie about Sally. Please, I think I should do that."

I was so eager to see Rosie I couldn't wait. I hope—No! I rejected the thought. No reason to panic, Rosie is fine. Everything is fine.

I found the KLM airline counter. Few people arrived as early as me, so almost immediately I was called up to the one-person stand. I presented my passport and ticket, and placed my suitcase on the scale attached to the side of the counter, fighting the temptation to claim it as carry-on luggage. A cobalt-uniformed young lady paused for a moment after glancing at the ticket. She didn't have to say anything; droll glints in her eyes told me something wasn't right. I was expecting the worst, but to my surprise, she swiped my passport through the reader after a few hundred clicks of the keyboard's keys, and returned my documents.

"Is everything all right?" I said.

"Yes, Mr. Clatt, everything is fine now. I'm sorry. I had to re-book your flight—luckily you have an open ticket. Boarding starts at four-fifteen, at gate number T-3. This is your seat," she said as she pointed, "thirty-six B; you're lucky—a few seats were still available. Next time, please call ahead. And thank you for choosing KLM," she said, handing me a boarding pass.

Call ahead? "I don't know what you mean, but of course. Yes, sure—thank you," I said, making room for an elderly woman with three suitcases, who must've spotted the boarding pass in my hand and started to push me out of the way.

* * *

The rattling air conditioner of the yellow cab wasn't doing its job well enough to keep me from sticking to the vinyl seat. One of these famous blistering spring days, I thought. Sure it's eighty, or so even now. And the humidity! Droplets of sweat fell from my forehead to my shirt every time the cab bounced over a pothole. The cabby's soft but off-key singing wasn't helping either. I was ready to jump out of the cab and run all the way to Fox River Valley Gardens.

Rosie was waiting for me. It was unquestionable, and I couldn't bear the thought that I wasn't there when she woke up. I should have been there for her. I hated my inability to be with Rosie, but at the same time, it was my duty to fulfill Sally's last request. Together these conflicting demands perplexed me and complicated my life, but I was finally able to acknowledge the importance of Sally's wish, of her desire to make me go to France. Rosie has been awakened and that was the most important outcome.

The sharp squeal of the cab's ailing brakes signaled our arrival at the hospital. Even before the cab came to a full stop, I threw two fifties at the driver and jumped out. I ran through the entrance door, dropping the idea of stopping by the reception desk, and caught the elevator. No one would care about the sticky visitor pass anyway; they never did, so I saved myself a little time. It took forever for the awkward lift to climb to the fourth floor.

In the middle of the corridor, a glass wall separated the ICU ward from the rest of the hospital. I tried the door and it clicked open for me. I ducked inside. As fast as I could, I flew through the lifeless hallway, and stormed through the Rosie's door. If I expected any reaction from her—my hopes were dashed.

Without the ominous sounds of the dismal machines by the headboard and on both sides of her bed, the room would have been filled with sinister stillness. Rosie lay exactly as I left her a few days ago. On her back, her hands penetrated by the life-sustaining IVs. Poor thing was exhausted from waiting. I'm going to sit down by her bed and wait until she wakes up. It shouldn't take long. She has to sleep through the trauma, sleep and rest as much as she can. I pulled a chair next to the bed and sat. I followed the steady rise and fall of her breathing beneath the pale bed sheets, and I waited.

"Here you are." Pete's voice rescued me from my thoughts. He stood in the doorway wearing khaki shorts and a light yellow polo that contrasted with his deep tan. "How have you been, Joe?"

"Shh…" I hissed. "Rosie is sleeping. Let's try not to wake her up. Not yet, I can wait. Let's talk outside." I tried to lead him out of the room.

I didn't like the guise of Pete's face. He wore an expressionless mask.

"I'm sorry, I think I'm tired," I said, trying to soften my abrupt words. "I was sure you'd get my message."

"I did," said Pete, slowly weighing each word. "And that's why I went to the airport, but I must have missed you."

"Why? It wasn't necessary. I asked you to meet me here," I said.

"Joe—"

"I wanted to see Rosie right away. I wanted to talk to her. I wanted to—" I pointed at my daughter. "She's sleeping now, but I hope you told her I was coming."

"Joe—"

"Pete, I hope you haven't told her about Sally," I said. "She knows that I only went away because of important business. Doesn't she?"

"Joe!" Pete took a few steps toward me. He grabbed my hands and kept them locked inside of his own. "Hold on, Joe. I couldn't talk to her, remember—" I hated the tone of his voice.

"What do you mean, you couldn't talk to her?"

"Joe, please don't get upset. I know you're having a hard time, but—"

"You're wrong. I was having a hard time. Now all that has changed. I know Rosie—"

"Listen, Joe," Pete sighed. "Rosie is…it's not good… she is still in a coma. She's been like that since you left a couple of months ago."

"Wait, wait, wait—" I said, when the meaning of his words finally filtered through. "What did you say?"

"Her condition got worse since you left two months ago." Pete's eyes drifted away from me as he spoke.

"Got worse. How it could be?" I drew out the words. Something wasn't right—I must've misheard. Why? How could she get worse? She's supposed to be fine. She—And— "You mean it has changed during…" I thought for a second, "… the last six days or so?"

Pete's warm, protective hands gripped mine even tighter, holding me in place.

"Son, believe me, please," he said. "You have been gone for two months—"

Then, even as I watched Pete's mouth open and close, the only voice I heard was the metallic sound of my daughter's heart monitor. I missed the moment when Pete let go of my hands, and I had to use the cold, rigid hospital wall for support when my legs became too weak to hold me up.

"What do you mean?" I whispered, looking straight into Pete's eyes. Either I was experiencing a temporary breakdown or I was just plain crazy. I leaned toward the latter.

"What do you mean?" I repeated a little louder this time.

"Joe," Pete grabbed my arms again, and held me like he knew the wall wasn't sufficient by itself. "It's July already." He paused. "The twenty-second of July."

Before the pulsating metallic sound filled up the room again, I thought I caught a glimpse of a large golden ring on Pete's finger.

Chapter 20

It took a long time for my mind to assimilate the unexplainable reality that I had missed two months of my life. Have I truly missed it? Who wouldn't be willing to give anything for the remote possibility of running into his lost love just one more time? Even if it meant…What did all of this mean? Did I perfectly lose myself while re-enacting an ancient legend? Was it only a recreation of the events, or something more? I didn't know. All I knew, was that I did what I had to do, and my goal should be to prepare myself to deal with the consequences.

Sequestered in Sally's room, I replayed all the scenes from my trip to Saintes-Maries-de-la-Mer in search of even the tiniest hint of an explanation that I could apply to rescue myself. I couldn't find anything. Nothing made sense to me. My thoughts spiraled around a woman, young at first, who resembled Sally, exactly as I remembered my wife, her transformation into an elderly being during our descent from the grotto, and then her disappearance in the church. Was it a church? I'm not sure. Who was that woman? Yet somehow, I knew it was Sally—I felt that.

But who was she? It seemed that everything pointed in one direction. But it was too—I wasn't ready to even contemplate this supposition. And then Saint Sara, whose statue I had the privilege of carrying. Wasn't she a little girl when she arrived in France? At least Jean-Paul said so. So why was the statue of a woman instead of a child? And who was Pierre, that skeleton-man Jean-Paul introduced me to? And, what about Jean-Paul, and his relationship to Pete? I didn't have the slightest idea. I thought that, in every single act of this staged play, I was not only a spectator but I was also an actor in one of the leading roles. I just couldn't get the director to tell me what my role was.

Back in the church, when I saw the lamenting child, I assumed it cried for its mother. Could that Sally really be this kid's mother? When she came to the crypt, she was too old, and the child too young, seven or eight at the most. But it seemed to be the same child I spotted on that bizarre boat, I thought. When I approached the subject from that perspective, and accepted the hypothesis that the whole occurrence was a symbol, a sign aimed at me to prove Rosie would be fine, then everything aligned itself in logical explanation. Until, of course I returned from France, and learned that Rosie's condition had deteriorated. That fact destroyed my theories.

I was exhausted from this fierce battle with my imagination, especially when I realized I had nothing to use to my advantage. I was doomed to lose. I finally understood I had to either accept reality as it was, or live in the deluded world of my own fantasies. To be honest, it wasn't an easy choice.

Pete took good care of me during that time, patiently waiting for my wounds to heal. I was thankful he didn't ask questions. I wasn't about to ask any either. I was frightened of answers. I vowed to myself never to speak about my trip to France with anyone, even with Pete. Especially with him. And I felt silent mutual understanding. I wanted to forget, to erase it from my memory, though the picture of that Sally was imprinted there forever.

"Do you think you could find some work for me, again?" I asked Pete during my first breakfast downstairs.

"Are you sure you want to go back this soon?" he said. "If you need more rest—"

"No, that's enough. I have to do something. Get out, see people," I said with determination. "I need to keep my mind occupied. That's what I need. I don't want to be any more of a burden than I already am."

"You're not a burden, Joe. You never will be," said Pete. "I'll ask. And I'm more than sure Steve will take you back, no matter what." Pete's voice betrayed him—he didn't have to ask; he must have been planning it, or at least preparing for this scenario. So I kept quiet, letting him play his game as he wished. My options were very limited.

I started the very next morning. As Pete predicted, Steve agreed to take me back without question. It appeared that he was still in need of a poorly qualified carpenter to help his crew with the most tedious tasks. Did he do it out of pity, or was he just trying to help? Or both? It didn't matter to me, not a bit. The most important thing for me was that he took me back. I missed being in the presence of these obliging people who didn't ask questions, and never demanded explanations, silent people whose one concern, I understood now, was not to hurt others, even outsiders. I knew by then even their sometimes questioning glances, were harmless—who wouldn't be curious in such situation. But in the end, they all treated me well. I felt grateful for such an approach, and tried to make sure they were aware I didn't mean to offend them in any way.

* * *

A sea of time has passed since I started to work for Steve again. Not much happened, just plenty of hard work with very few unoccupied moments. I got used to the routine, and even though each day seemed to be nearly identical, I didn't complain.

"We're going to start a new house tomorrow," said Frank, as we finished one day. Frank was officially promoted to a supervisor position during the time I was gone. And he was as proud of it as one could ever be. "You'll be working on it with Brian."

"But we're not done with this one yet," I said. "There's plenty of cleanup to be done."

"I know." He pointed to the group gathering slowly by his truck. "Thanks to those lazy bastards."

"Oh, yeah?" said one of them

"That hurts!" said Brian.

"Hurts?" Frank laughed. "You'll see how it hurts when I cut checks for you on Friday."

"OK, OK, boss, but it isn't our fault," Brian said, trying to defend the crew. "It was—"

"Like always," said Frank, cutting him short. "So both of you will start on a new project, and those losers", he directed his finger toward the group, "will try to wrap it up here. And I hope they can finally do some work."

"What are we going to do?" I said.

"Just a little kitchen and the bathroom. I need you to start taking everything out. The dumpster should be there in the morning."

"Is there enough room to put it in the yard?" I said. "Remember the last time—we got a ticket for leaving it on the street."

"Don't worry," said Frank. "The driveway is deep enough. The only thing that bothers me is it won't look very appealing for people who go to church."

"A church?" I felt a chilling sensation. That church? Not too far where Sally and Rosie… I hope I can do this.

"Oh, yeah. Didn't I tell you? This is like the third or fourth house from the church. Everyone who passes by will get a shot at our mess." He paused. "But it will only be for a week, maybe two. We should be able to keep it clean enough, but, knowing the speed that all of you are working, I doubt it." He waved his hand. "We should be OK, I hope," he added with a smile.

We started early in the next morning and by late afternoon, we had finished tearing apart the built-in cabinets, and removed the ancient yellow tiles that seemed to be stuck on with super glue. We did more than expected on the first day, and the stripped rooms bore witness to our efforts. Nevertheless, we managed to finish earlier than planned. Brian had already left, and I was about to drive to the hospital to visit Rosie as I had every day for nearly the last six months. At the last second, I made a sharp turn, and drove my truck through the wrought-iron gate that commanded me inside the churchyard. It was the first time since my visit to France that I had come close to any church. I had no idea what made me stop there. I sat in the truck for a while, my radio turned off, before I decided how to proceed.

I grabbed the bronze handle of its massive entrance door, and automatically noticed St. Mary Magdalene Church sign carved in the stone. I had hoped the gate would be closed, but it swung open. A few lighted candles by one of the altars, and light filtered by slender stained glass windows were enough to maneuver safely within. I stood by the door for a moment, and then an indiscernible force drew me into one of the wooden pews nearby. There I reflected before the ornate main altar.

It was an unfamiliar feeling for me. It wasn't invocation— I just sat there letting my thoughts become acquainted with the spirits. I wasn't afraid anymore. For some reason I wasn't able to explain, I felt like it was decided already, a long time ago—I have been forgiven, accepted, and welcomed. When I left, I already promised I would be back here tomorrow.

I tried to get back and sit in the church every day since then. Even when we finished the house nearby, I continued to stop at the church on my way to see Rosie. The only exception was on Sundays. I couldn't force myself to go—too many sorry faces around made me angry. I preferred the empty church when no one was around, and I was left to myself.

Every time I went back there, I found myself taking a seat closer to the altar. It wasn't planned, nor was I more courageous to move forward; rather, I felt like I was being granted permission to come nearer.

The prayers came unexpectedly. They were not the memorized formulas written and taught from the religious books in confirmation classes. I didn't remember those; I didn't think I have ever learned anything more than the "Our Father," anyway. I made my own, right then on the spot. I wasn't sure if they were even appropriate. What intrigued me the most was that I was able to leave all my emotions behind. It was spontaneous, unintended. I discovered I didn't need to ask for anything, not even for the things I wanted most. I was astounded to find myself connecting with God and not expect anything in return.

A couple of months before, the self-important doctors had written Rosie off after yet another abrupt change in her condition.

They ripped away the last shreds of hope by diagnosing irreversible damage in her brain. They predicted she would never wake up from the coma.

"You have to understand, Mr. Clatt," said one of them, "even if she was to wake up, which is impossible according to our diagnosis, the damage to her brain is so extensive, she wouldn't be able to function normally. Please understand that. She is kept alive only by life support equipment. Her brain is dying every second. I'm sorry."

"What do you suggest?" I said nervously. "You don't think I'll agree to—"

"From my personal point of view, it would be best for her, but of course…"

But how could I? I didn't want to admit there was nothing I could do; these self-appointed gods had passed judgment, but how could I even think about accepting something like that? I couldn't. I wanted to fight. I wanted to take Rosie out of their clutches and carry her to a safe place where she could heal.

It was one of the warmest evenings that late spring, just ten months since I visited France—May 24. As I stood to leave the cool, soothing church, I spotted a man in the back. Someone is here—he must have just arrived. I rarely saw anyone else during all the time here, apart from the shadow of the priest running through the church as if he became undetectable. As I approached the pew the man was sitting in, he stepped in front of me.

"Pete? I didn't recognize you," I said. "What's going on? How did you find me?"

"Come, come quickly!" He didn't listen to me, tugging my arm insistently.

And then the most horrible scenario flashed through my mind. Rosie! They had been trying to prepare me. God! I couldn't move; I didn't even feel Pete pushing me inside the car. Help me. Please. I can't take it.

"Joe, Joe. Get in!" I heard his faint voice. "We have to go. Now! They just called from the hospital."

Epilogue

It was precisely a year to the day, July 22, 2001, after Joe returned from his visit to Saintes-Maries-de-la-Mer when he found himself walking the familiar path of sorrows again. The Fox River Valley Gardens Cemetery was indecently sunny and bursting with life. He didn't need a guide, he knew his way too well. He had spent countless hours there, sitting alone, trying to put into words every little detail of what had happened in his life since Sally left. But this was the moment he hadn't imagined, even in his wildest dreams. It was so abstract, unreachable, and beyond Joe's control, he still couldn't accept the fact it was happening. With all the hope he had thrown away, the forgotten silent wishes, the hours spent by the altar, he had made reconciliation with the inevitable. Now Joe slowly strolled toward his wife's final resting place.

He squeezed that hand yet another time, trying to convince himself that everything was real. Reality doesn't mean anything. It's overrated, he told himself.

"Are you ready, honey?" Joe had asked a little more than half an hour ago when Rosie was being released from the hospital.

"I am," she said, sitting on the edge of the hospital bed.

"Are you feeling—"

"I'm fine, Dad. You heard it yourself."

"I know, I know. Just asking." Joe waved his hand in the air.

"Dad?" said Rosie after a moment of silence. She was stuffing the last few books into a large duffel bag.

"Yes?"

"Are we going to Grandpa's?"

"You know. I...we live there now. He can't wait to see you home. I suspect he is going to throw a welcome back party for you." Joe stepped closer to the bed, seeing shadows of anxiety on Rosie's face. "Is something wrong?"

"No, No!" said Rosie. "It's just—" Rosie paused.

"What is it, honey? Tell me if you don't want a party, I call him now. He just wanted the best."

"It's not that," she said, looking out of the window.

"Then what is it? I can see something is bothering you. Tell me what it is."

"Oh, nothing, Dad." Rosie's eyes moved away from the window, and rested at Joe. "I was just wondering if we could see Mom on our way home."

Joe turned his head away. During the whole time Rosie had to spend in the hospital, they had never talked about Sally. He wanted to tell her the whole truth right after Rosie's unanticipated awakening from the coma, but he simply couldn't.

Rosie's recovery was a miracle. It wasn't a miracle like you see in the movies—Rosie didn't just jump out of bed shouting, "I'm cured!" But it was a miracle nevertheless. It didn't matter that she had to stay under constant medical observation for nearly two months. Her strength had to be re-grown within herself, her ability to function normally taught from the basics. It was a challenging task for both of them, but Joe never heard one complaint from Rosie.

With gritted teeth and a soft smile of determination in her eyes, she continued her laborious task of bringing herself back to the world of the living. Even before the bewildered doctors told him so, Joe knew she would successfully recover. He had known since the first glance at Rosie's face when he arrived at the hospital the day Pete dragged him from the church. Rosie's eyes wordlessly told him her objective, and he had faith in her. She was Sally's daughter, and her intent look had only proved the obvious to him.

But this one thing constantly bothered Joe from the time that Rosie was able to construct short, simple sentences. She actually never asked about Sally, not even once. It seemed like she knew and didn't want to talk about it. Joe made certain that Pete, the doctors—everyone who encountered her—hadn't discussed anything with Rosie. He wanted to talk to Rosie about her mom's death, but puzzled, he took the doctor's advice and didn't say a word until Rosie was ready to make the first step.

Joe also decided to keep his trip to France a secret—for the moment at least. He was confident he would tell Rosie about it at some point. When she got her strength back, she would fully grasp the meaning of what he wanted to say to her. The last thing Joe wanted was to heap yet another burden on Rosie's precarious shoulders, as if her life wasn't eventful enough already. Rosie was mature for her age; sometimes he thought maybe she was too advanced. But some things, he thought, had to be handed out with moderation, just to make sure she wouldn't get too agitated.

Something had planted itself inside Joe's mind the first day he had seen Rosie awaken. A tiny grain of uncertainty, a slight impression that Rosie was hiding something from him, began to grow. Joe couldn't help feeling that it wasn't only him Rosie held back from. It seemed she had locked something away from everyone, including herself. After days had passed, he dismissed the thought, and like everything else, he blamed it on the trauma and on his own exaggerated perception of his daughter.

"Dad?" said Rosie aloud. "Did you hear me? I said I want to——"

"I did, Rosie, I did," said Joe. "But I thought we would go there tomorrow."

"Dad?"

"Let's go home now—Pete can't wait to see you."

"It won't take long, and Grandpa won't mind, I know."

"Aren't you tired?" said Joe, examining his fingernails.

"Dad?" Rosie's smile struck Joe right in the middle of his chest. It was as if he could see Sally in front of him. "Tired of what?"

He couldn't get over the resemblance, staring at his daughter with his mouth half open.

"Dad?" Rosie pulled Joe's hand. "Dad! Are you listening to me?"

"Yes, Rosie. I'm sorry," he said.

"I'm starting to wonder who the sick person is when you act like that." Rosie smiled. "What is it with you?"

"Nothing, honey, I'm just exhausted. If you really want to go, that's fine with me. Let's go." Joe turned around. "I'm sure Pete won't be happy, but he'll understand if we come a little later."

"Thanks, Daddy," said Rosie.

"Wait! We don't have any flowers. I didn't buy—I thought we would go there tomorrow. We have to stop—"

"Dad, don't panic. Mom doesn't need flowers. She needs…us."

Joe watched his daughter. Another strange woman. It looks like I am lucky to be dominated by such, he thought.

"What's wrong, Daddy?" asked Rosie when they pulled up to the empty cemetery parking lot after the silent ride. She had even turned off the radio, and rolled down the window to let the wind comb her red hair.

"Nothing—" said Joe. He captured Rosie's hand as they started to walk. "It's not the happiest place I know." After a few quiet steps, he added, "But it seems I can't live without it."

Joe walked automatically; he had that route permanently engraved in his heart. He observed Rosie carefully as they wandered through the maze of monuments, and he caught something unpredictable in his daughter's appearance. Confused, he observed Rosie smiling. It was a smile of an excited child who was about to open a gift found under the Christmas tree. So innocent yet so filled with expectation. By the time they finally made it to Sally's grave, Rosie was blooming.

"Dad, what is it with you?" Rosie stood next to her mother's headstone. "Are you OK? You don't look too good, Daddy."

"I'm fine," said Joe. "It's just a—"

"Oh, I know what it is." Rosie's face illuminated even more. "You're shocked that I'm not crying."

"It's not about crying."

"So, what's it about then?"

"You look like you are—" Joe couldn't say it.

"Happy?" Rosie cocked her head at her father.

"Yes, happy," his voice sounded harsh at first, but then he softened his tone. "Aren't you even a little—"

"Dad, let me tell you something." Rosie's little eyes unsuccessfully tried to meet Joe's—tears clouded his vision.

What is it with her? She behaves like an adult, he thought. And I was sure that this was my little girl. Who needs the help here? And he said aloud, "Go ahead, Rosie. I'm listening."

"Mom's been away for more than a year and a half now. Hasn't she?"

"What about it?"

"I couldn't be here until now, could I?"

"You were in the hospital—"

"So don't you think that when a daughter visits her mother after such a long time, she should be happy when they finally get together?"

"Rosie—" Joe stepped back. "Your mom is dead, this is a cemetery—"

"What does that mean? That I have to cry? Dad, I'm just happy to be here with Mom, and I know that she feels the same way."

Joe nervously clasped his hands together. "Rosie, I have never told you about this before. I thought it could wait."

"Dad—"

"Sally, your mom has—"

"Dad, please—"

"Rosie, I know everything, I have seen—"

"Dad?!" Rosie's voice was a demand for immediate attention rather than a shout.

"What, honey?" Joe stared at her. "If you don't want to talk about it, I understand."

"It's not that," Rosie moved away from Joe. "Dad, you only think you know everything." Joe heard a soft whisper.

He stood to the side of Sally's grave, trying to find the meaning in his daughter's words. A split second later, even his thoughts ceased to function, like someone flipped an invisible switch. On her knees with her hands wrapped around the marble obelisk, Rosie cuddled up to the rock, her contour indistinguishable, her hair veiling her face.

"Aemaa," she whispered. "Aemaa."

Acknowledgments

I would like to thank Deborah Cullins-Smith for her help and support and Maciej Danek for allowing me to draw on one of his many amazing poems.

About the Author

Greg M. Sarwa was born in Chrzanow, Poland. He currently lives in Illinois with his wife and two daughters.

The Valley of Silent People is his third novel. *If only I could...,* his second book, has been named a runner-up in USA Book News *The National "Best Books 2007"* Awards in Fiction and Literature, Romance category. His first, entitled *The Cattle*, has been awarded the 2005 Book of the Year Bronze Medal in Science Fiction by ForeWord Magazine.

Visit www.gregsarwa.com